Her Wild Irish Rogue
A Legend to Love

Saralee Etter

To
Terry
and
Clayton

1

"Surely the Duke will be there today," Captain Stephen Killian muttered.

Lieutenant Leary adjusted the reins in his hand as he drove the borrowed phaeton down the wide Parisian avenue toward the Duke of Wellington's temporary headquarters. The horses were borrowed, too, a pair of bone-setters but the best he could find in the war-weary city. Leary risked a quick glance at his friend and gave a non-committal shrug.

Captain Killian, fresh and crisp in his full regimental uniform despite the summer warmth, cracked his knuckles. "It's been a month since Waterloo, and Paris is in the hands of the Allies. I need something to do. Surely he'll have time to see me. Give me new orders."

"Surely he will," echoed Leary comfortingly. The horses tossed their heads nervously as they passed a field with Prussians practicing shooting drills. The fabled City of Light was overrun with soldiers from a dozen nations, camping in every city park, eating their heads off and swaggering around town looking for amusement. The new regime of Louis the Eighteenth had barely settled back in power after Napoleon's second exile to the distant island of St. Helena.

They had just reached the Bridge of Jena, *le Pont d'Iena*, as the French called it, when Killian shouted, "Stop the phaeton!"

"What is it?" Leary barely had time to pull the horses to a stop before his friend had jumped down. He watched open-mouthed as Killian sprinted toward the bridge. "Ah, bless ye for a madman, Stephen Killian, what mischief are ye up to now?"

On the bridge, two Prussian soldiers were stacking sticks of dynamite at each of the pilings. A third Prussian was unspooling a long wire fuse from the explosives toward the detonator, hidden behind stacks of sandbags on the riverbank.

Killian drew his sword as he ran shouting at the trio of soldiers on the bridge. Two of them dropped their sticks of dynamite and backed away in confusion. The third solider, the one with the spool of wire, held his ground. With a yell, Killian lunged at him, his cavalry sword whistling dangerously through the air before the fellow's face. Shielding himself with his forearm, the soldier stepped back, tripped over a pile of explosives, and fell down.

Leary sighed. "Ah, fighting to put an end to the war. It's mad as a hatter, he is." He leaned forward to rest his forearm on one knee, holding the carriage reins loosely in one hand as he watched the melee. He had witnessed his friend's fearsome battle fury and knew Killian wasn't in any danger. But the war was over now, and it was not up to Killian to prevent other soldiers from continuing the war's destruction.

A Prussian officer in a gold-epauletted uniform began screaming angrily in German. The officer's high forehead and the beak of a nose over luxuriant mustaches identified him as Field Marshal Gebhard von Blücher.

At Blücher's direction, two more soldiers drew their swords and advanced on Killian. With a wild laugh, Killian sprang forward to meet both at once. Their swords clanged together and then slid apart with a steely rasp as the three combatants engaged and then danced free. Killian was light on his feet and deceptively strong despite his slender build. A lock of dark hair fell over his forehead as Killian slashed at first one and then the other, feinting and parrying, his blade flickering in the sunlight as if on fire. Their shouts soon became grunts of effort as, slowly but surely, Killian drove the Prussian swordsmen down the bridge.

The soldier with the spool of wire had picked himself up and gone back to his work. Crawling along the ground, nearly trampled by the swordsmen, he attaché d one end of the fuse to a stick of dynamite. He unspooled the wire as he backed carefully toward the detonator hidden among the sandbags.

Killian noticed him and shouted a curse. "You fool! Do you mean to blow all of us up?"

One of the Prussians saw the danger too. He roared to his companion, gesturing toward the soldier laying the wire. The other Prussian turned and slashed at the kneeling soldier, who cringed back.

On the riverbank, Blücher waved his arms at the soldiers and shouted. The second swordsman stopped attacking the man with the wire and rejoined the fight with Killian. The three-way duel raged on as the two swordsmen pushed Killian back, forcing him to retreat to the highest part of the bridge.

An open barouche pulled up beside Leary. It held four passengers: a British officer, a civilian gentleman, and two ladies, whose faces were hidden by bonnets and the ruffled parasols they carried to ward off any errant ray of sun.

The gold medals on the British officer's scarlet frock coat glinted in the sunlight as he rose from his seat in the barouche. He had a long, lean face and a high-bridged nose. Dark eyes sparkled under bushy brows as he surveyed the commotion on the bridge.

He called to Leary. "You there! What's going on?"

Leary nodded respectfully to the Duke of Wellington. "The Prussians will be wishing to blow up the bridge, your Grace," Leary called back. "Begorra, and isn't it our own Captain Killian who is preventing them."

The ruffled parasols fluttered as the ladies gasped with shock.

"What?" roared the Duke. He clambered down from the carriage and stalked toward the Prussian general. "Curse it, Blücher! You can't just go about blowing bridges up. The war's over."

Leary nodded to himself, satisfied that the Duke would settle the situation.

Wellington turned to the combatants on the bridge. "Halt! Swords up, now!"

All three swordsmen stopped, their sword points whipping straight up. Killian stepped back smartly and stood at attention. The Prussians, glancing from Blücher to Wellington, wavered uncertainly between instinctive obedience to a command and their desire to finish the fight.

"Now explain what this is all about, General von Blücher,"

Wellington demanded.

Red-faced, Blücher turned to Wellington. "I shall rid the earth of this – this abomination, this disgrace!"

Wellington surveyed the bridge critically. "It's a bridge. What's disgraceful about it?"

"Do you know what they call it? Do you?" Blücher shouted. "That monster, that despicable, vile, repulsive—"

As Blücher's speech disintegrated into strangled German curses, Wellington nodded. "Yes, yes. Napoleon. Go on."

"He named this bridge the *Pont d'Iena!*" Blücher snarled. "After the battle of Jena! Jena, where twenty thousand of my brave soldiers were swarmed under and destroyed, slaughtered by that villain's foul scum! My men! Twenty thousand fine, honest Prussian fathers and sons. I swear to you by all that's holy, there will be no smug monuments to that heartbreaking disaster. I will erase this disgusting bridge from the face of the earth. I will—"

"Blücher!" Wellington shook his head. "It's time to stop."

"I shall stop. After I blow up this bridge." Blücher turned and barked an order to the Prussians on the bridge, waving them back to solid ground. The soldier who had laid the fuse connected the wire to the detonator. A Prussian engineer stepped up behind the plunger.

Only Killian was left standing at attention on the bridge. He didn't move. Chin lifted, eyes straight ahead, he stood silently amid the piles of dynamite.

"Ah, Killian, curse ye for the devil's own fool! Get out of there!" shouted Leary.

Captain Killian flashed a smile at his friend. He shook his head, then went back to staring straight ahead. Passersby gawked at the scene as they walked or rode past, crossing themselves piously, but still hurrying along their way.

One of the ladies in the carriage stood up. Leary caught a glimpse of dark curls as she called out, "Your Grace, you can't let them blow it up with our soldier still on the bridge!"

As she spoke, a dandified old French gentleman who had been limping along the promenade with the aid of a gold-tipped black cane stopped and raised his quizzing glass to look at her. The dark-haired young lady beckoned to him, at which he bowed and limped over to Wellington's carriage. His male servant followed at his elbow.

The old Frenchman was elegantly dressed in satin and

lace, his pale, pain-lined face framed by an old-fashioned powdered wig. Leary only heard the rising lilt of his question and the lady's anxious tone as she replied. A few more murmured words, and then the servant sprinted off.

At the bridge, the Duke of Wellington glared at the Prussian general. "If you kill my man, it will mean war between Britain and Prussia, Blücher."

Silently, General Blücher glared back at Wellington. The Prussian's jaw was tight, and his eyes shone with unshed tears.

The old French gentleman limped up to them. "Ah, good morning, *mes amis*. Is not the weather fine this day? Paris, she is so beautiful in the morning. And at twilight. All the time, in fact. Paris is the queen of cities."

He smiled warmly upon the two generals. The thick, angry tension between them broke, and both men drew in deep breaths. They greeted the newcomer, Wellington doffing his black bicorne and Blücher clicking his booted heels together.

"Monsieur Talleyrand," said Wellington curtly. "Taking a morning walk? Please do not let us detain you."

The old French foreign minister raised his eyebrows politely. "Not at all, my dear General. I am waiting here for the so-distinguished Tsar Alexander. I expect him shortly."

Talleyrand looked out past the long, graveled promenade, as if waiting for the Tsar. On the other side of the promenade, a line of trees hid the Prussian encampments on the Champs de Mars from their view. All of the open fields of Paris had been turned into bivouacs for the British, Russian, Prussian, Austrian, Italian and other conquerors, who had jointly defeated Napoleon and now controlled France. Somewhere in the distance lay the headquarters of the Tsar of All Russia.

"Tsar Alexander?" Blücher echoed.

The Frenchman's eyes twinkled. "He will be surprised, no doubt, to see you here. But he will be delighted, naturally."

"What have you got up your sleeve, Monsieur?" Wellington demanded.

Talleyrand lifted his quizzing glass to his eye and surveyed the bridge. Killian still stood at attention amid the piles of dynamite connected by a long wire fuse to the detonator on the riverbank.

Oh, là là," the French minister said with a mild cluck of

his tongue. "What is that dynamite for?"

"I am blowing up this bridge," Blücher announced. "It is an insult to all of Prussia."

Talleyrand nodded mournfully. "My heart goes out to you, Herr General. I sympathize completely. Just to hear that bridge's name spoken, ah, it tears at the soul."

"It does?" Blücher said blankly. He blinked and nodded. "Yes, it does."

"Do you want him to dynamite the bridge?" Wellington asked, outraged. "I refuse to permit it! My man is stationed on the bridge to prevent it!"

"Yes, my dear Wellington, please do prevent it," Talleyrand begged. "It would be such a pity if Tsar Alexander were to come here for the bridge re-naming ceremony, only to find there was no more bridge to re-name."

Wellington and Blücher both turned their heads slowly to stare at Talleyrand.

"Bridge. Re-naming. Ceremony?" Wellington repeated.

"Vat is zis bridge re-naming ceremony?" Frustration deepened Blücher's accent. "I vas not informed of any bridge re-naming ceremony!"

"Oh but yes," Talleyrand exclaimed, looking from one to the other with an expression of dismayed innocence. "Of course, the bridge cannot continue to bear a name which is so offensive to our Prussian friends. We must have peace. And so, Tsar Alexander will arrive, the bridge will be given a new name, *et voilà!*"

The famed diplomat spread wide the fingers of his left hand, while his right hand gripped the gold handle of his ebony cane. Despite the smile on the old Frenchman's putty-colored face, Leary could see a weary tightness in the satin-clad shoulders.

At that moment, the sound of clopping hooves and jingling harnesses preceded the appearance of Tsar Alexander of Russia himself, followed by retinue of fierce-looking Russian Cossacks.

Upon seeing the two generals and Talleyrand, the Tsar dismounted lightly. Tall and fit, he had an air of energy and determination. He looked impatiently from one to the other before asking, "Well?"

Talleyrand said quickly, "Your Imperial Highness, thank you so much for coming. We are agreed, are we not, that this bridge should henceforth be known by a different name?"

The Tsar's eyes narrowed slightly. "Yes?"

"It would be my humble suggestion," Talleyrand pursued, "That since the building closest to the bridge on the other side is the Military School, this bridge should be called the *Pont de l'École Militaire*. No doubt your Excellency can see the merit of my suggestion."

As the French diplomat was speaking, the Tsar looked over the bridge, taking in the dynamite, the sandbags, and Captain Killian standing on the bridge. "What is going on here?"

"Your Imperial Highness, I did not know that you were planning this – this renaming ceremony," Blücher said gruffly. "The Prussian people will not allow themselves to be insulted by a bridge which exalts the barbaric slaughter of our soldiers."

"The British people will not stand idly by while the Prussians begin the war all over again," Wellington snapped. "There must be no more wanton destruction."

The Tsar nodded. "Ah." With military precision, he turned to Talleyrand. "Let the renaming ceremony begin."

Talleyrand spread his hands. "*Mais oui.* One moment, if you please."

At that moment the Frenchman's servant rushed up to him, panting, and held out a bottle of champagne. Then Talleyrand gave a short speech which somehow connected bridges to international peace, and handed the champagne bottle to the Tsar. "If you would do the honors, your Imperial Highness."

"Is that how it's done, christening a bridge as one does a ship?" the Tsar asked doubtfully. "Very well, then. I christen thee *Le Pont de l'École Militaire.*"

After the champagne bottle had duly been smashed against the bridge, the Tsar mounted up. "Clean up this mess," he ordered, pointing at the explosives and wires. Then the Tsar of all Russia trotted off, trailing Cossacks.

"He got champagne on my dynamite," grumbled Blücher.

Wellington gestured at Killian. "Come down off the Pont de l'École Militaire, soldier. Our work here is done." Wiping his hands together, he strode back to his barouche.

Captain Killian grinned as he approached the Duke and his party in the barouche. "Faith, and it's thanking you I must be, your Grace, for saving my life."

"Your brave action was commendable, though somewhat reckless," Wellington said. "What's your name and rank, sir?"

Killian introduced himself, then took a deep breath. "If it's not too bold, your Grace, I was hoping to continue to serve you. And our country as well. If you'd be having a need for an aide, an assistant, to perform even the least service for you, I'm your man."

At Killian's words, the older man in the carriage snorted derisively, and then covered it with a cough. Leary disliked him on sight. The fellow had the kind of bland, unremarkable appearance that made him hard to remember. His well-tailored suit was dark brown, matching the mud of Paris. His face was a pale oval with barely distinguishable eyebrows over small, deep-set eyes. From time to time, a tiny fraction of pink tongue darted out from between his thin lips, like that of a snake testing the air.

The two ladies had set aside their parasols and Leary was able to get a better look at both of them. Both were young, and looked alike enough to be sisters. The quiet one was blonde, with a sweet expression that captivated Leary immediately. The dark-haired one, undeniably beautiful with her green eyes and dark hair, had more presence. Her regal expression contrasted with the frivolous pink pelisse she wore over a matching gown. Her green eyes were fixed on Killian.

The Duke of Wellington shook his head. "Ah. Thank you, Captain Killian, but we need not ask more of you. Those who witnessed you in battle said you were an extraordinarily fierce fighter, but they expressed concerns. When you were in the grip of your battle fury, you didn't seem to know anyone friend or foe. In short, you lose your head. Now is the time for diplomacy and strategy, when other skills are called for. You've earned your rest, my good man."

"Sure, and I can't be resting!" Killian burst out. "'Tis that I must do something. I'm not made for idleness. And I can behave like a gentleman if the occasion calls for it. My foster father is the Earl of Ulster. He sent me to Oxford, where I read classics. Beshrew me, I'm as learned and cultured as any man."

Wellington raised his eyebrows. "Impressive. But still I say

—"

The older man spoke in a smooth, insinuating voice. "Your Grace, perhaps Madame Scatha might be able to instruct the youth? Send him to her, and we shall see what use she can make of him."

The dark-haired beauty gasped, and all eyes turned to her. "No! Papa, you can't be serious! A man with a hot temper could get himself killed in Scatha's service. Not to mention that he could plunge all of Europe into the devil of a mess."

"Emma," the snakelike Lord Forgall said in a stern voice. "You forget yourself."

"Your point is well taken my dear," Wellington said to her. "But you must allow us to decide for ourselves. Madame Scatha....that is indeed a thought, Lord Forgall."

"Who is Madame Scatha?" Killian interrupted.

Lord Forgall smiled at Killian. "She assists us in diplomatic matters. Very sensitive matters. Quite subtle and delicate. But this work would require great self-control on your part. So if you're not up to it..."

"I'll do it," Killian cut in. "Whatever you might ask of me, I will learn. And I will succeed."

"That's the spirit, my boy," Lord Forgall said in that quiet, slightly amused voice. The tip of his pink tongue flickered at the corner of his mouth. "Here's Madame Scatha's direction. You may wish to visit her salon tomorrow."

"You won't be sorry, your Grace, my lord," Killian assured both the Duke and Lord Forgall. He bowed deeply to them both.

After the Duke and his companions had gone, Killian jumped into the phaeton beside his friend. "Did you hear that, Leary? This is the luckiest day of my life!"

"Is it, now?" Leary replied doubtfully, and urged the horses forward.

2

The sun was streaming through the tall windows of the small parlor where Miss Emma Forgall generally worked. Though most people thought that her work involved the normal tasks assigned to a young lady, such as managing the household and handling the polite correspondence with friends and acquaintances, Emma's particular delight in puzzles and numbers had led her father to teach her how to write and decipher codes. Now, after years of practice, Emma was the one person her father relied upon to decipher the secret communications that filtered through his department.

There were other cryptographers, of course, but none who could be at Lord Forgall's beck and call, none who were so thoroughly trusted by him. This was both a blessing and a curse, in Emma's opinion. A blessing because her father's reliance on her good work made her feel valuable to him. A curse, because she didn't know if he would ever allow her to live a life of her own choosing. What if she wanted to be free?

This morning, as she had watched that wild and reckless young captain battling a pair of Prussian soldiers on the bridge, she had been struck by how independent he seemed. No one had ordered him to defend that bridge. He had just chosen to risk his life in that fashion. His life had balanced on the edge of a knife, and he had chosen to put himself there. It had been frightening and even a bit foolish, but for a few moments she had wished she could do the same. Danger and victory! What could be more exciting?

But instead of a wild adventure, Emma, dutiful Emma,

spent several hours seated at the little table round table in the center of the room, decoding the communiqués that her father had asked her to work on. She was on the next-to-last one when she ran across some fascinating information from a certain regimental commander.

SPECIAL COMMENDATION RECOMMENDED FOR ROBERT LOCKSLEY'S EXTREME BRAVERY IN BATTLE. REFUSES TRAVEL TO PARIS, PREFERS RETURN TO NOTTINGHAM SOONEST.

A smile of delight spread over her face as she decoded this message. She knew this Robert Locksley, because he was her cousin—she'd known him all her life. Her father had trained him for years, hoping Robert would eventually one day step into his shoes. But Robert had refused that honor, and Lord Parkington had insinuated himself into his vacated position.

Instead, Robert had ended up on the battlefield, both a soldier and a spy, under the command of the very person who had sent this message. Their regiment had suffered heavy casualties, and she had despaired for his life. But now, this message had given her hope. Not only had Robert acted bravely enough to earn a commendation, but he was still alive. How typical of him to want to return home instead of coming to Paris to receive his commendation at the hands of his uncle!

She sat back with a sigh. How she missed Robert. It had been years since she had last seen him. Come to think of it, years had passed since she'd seen so many of her friends. Friends in Portugal whom she hadn't seen in two years now, and friends from Miss Prism's Academy for Young Ladies outside of London whom she hadn't seen in over three years. She wondered how Marianne Maidland was these days.

Actually, now that she thought of it, Marianne was from Nottingham, just like Robert was. So many young men had died in battle. Marianne would probably be delighted to know that Robert was still alive.

She stood up, and stretched her back after the hours of sitting hunched over her work. She stacked the papers neatly, and looked up as the maid Sophie entered. "The post, *Mademoiselle.*"

Emma sorted quickly through the letters. Most would go to her father, and the rest to her aunt, Madame Scatha. There were no letters for her today. But surely Marianne would be delighted to receive a letter from her. Emma and Marianne had become fast friends at Miss Prism's Young Ladies' Academy.

Miss Prism's Academy was located in the green rolling hills outside of London, which the headmistress had insisted was a healthful environment for young ladies. Emma, a city girl all her life, had enjoyed the mathematics classes while Marianne, raised in Sherwood Forest, had been a star in the sport of archery. Despite their differences, they had become fast friends. Emma had enjoyed some of the outdoor adventures Marianne had taken her on, although Marianne had never acquired an equal fascination with mathematics.

It had been a sad moment when Emma's father had taken her and and her younger sister Fiona out of school to go with him to Portugal. She and Marianne had exchanged letters, Emma sharing what she could of the foreign countries she had traveled to, and Marianne telling her amusing stories drawn from her own life. It was Emma's turn to write, anyway, and it was nice to have a bit of good news to share.

Emma's eye was caught by the stack of papers on the table. She sat back down to finish decoding the final communiqué before she indulged in the pleasure of writing her friend a letter.

Several minutes later, she realized that this communiqué required a different key in order to be decoded. This one was an old-fashioned system, using a book cipher, and the book she needed was in her father's safe room. How annoying. Well, she would take these finished ones up to the safe room to be locked up, and find the book she needed to finish her final task.

She carried the stack of secret communiqués upstairs to the safe room, which was where all important papers were locked up. The safe room was a small, windowless closet in the center of Madame Scatha's house. The door was hidden among the paneling, not easy for a casual observer to see. Emma turned the wooden molding that served as the door handle, but it was locked. Exasperated she knocked.

"Hello? Who is in there?"

A muffled voice came from inside the room. "Go away! Come back later."

Emma sighed. "Lord Parkington, I need to put these papers in there now. They must be locked up. My father said

—"

The door opened a crack. Lord Parkington's face was partially visible through the opening, and his voice was annoyed. "Do go away. I have important work to do. Come back later."

"But you know my father said to always lock up—"

"Can't you see I'm busy? Go put them on desk in the study for now. When I'm done, you can return them to this room." The door shut.

Emma called, "But my father says –"

"Go away!"

Exasperated, Emma marched to her father's study, which was a pleasant room with a big globe and many bookcases. This room looked like the place where an important official would do his work, but in fact it was mostly meant for ordinary business, and not for the secret work. Madame used it from time to time. There really was no reason why she could not leave the papers in the study just for a little while, until Lord Parkington had finished whatever it was that he was doing.

Emma slid the papers under the blotter on the big walnut desk, so they would not be too visible. Her duty done for the moment, she went back to her bedroom to write her letter to Marianne.

Her sister Fiona was in the bedroom, embroidering some linens. Setting her needle down carefully, she asked, "Finished with your work already?"

"For the moment," Emma said, seating herself at the small writing desk in their room and pulling out some sheets of letter-writing paper, an ink-pot and a quill. "Parkington has blockaded himself in the safe room and won't let me in, blast him."

"Emma! What sort of language is that for a lady?" Fiona said, scandalized.

She hunched a shoulder. "Well, who knows what he's doing in there. And I needed that volume of Horace—"

"But that's no reason to curse," Fiona said. "What will people think?"

Emma smiled at her. "Well there's no one here but you, and I already know what you think. Never mind that. I've got good news!"

Marianne clapped her hands together with a cry of delight.

"Oh, I love good news! What is it?"

"Cousin Robert is alive."

"How do you know?"

"It was in one of the communiques." Emma leaned over her paper and began to write.

My dear Marianne,

I hope you are happy and well in Nottingham. We are enjoying Paris very much. The French fashions are quite scandalous. You may not believe it, but ladies here are wearing flesh-toned pantaloons made of a light stockinet, extending all the way down to their ankles, beneath their sheer muslin dresses! The first time we saw a woman dressed in this fashion, both Fiona and I burst into a fit of the giggles. And of course, Papa asked us what the joke was, and we could hardly tell him!

Also, waists are higher and hemlines wider than in England. My Aunt Odile absolutely refused to allow Fiona and me to be seen in public in our "ridiculous English dresses" and immediately conveyed us to her modiste. Now we are suitably "a la mode" without being too French (no flesh-colored pantaloons for us!)

I know that you will remember my cousin Robert Locksley. When we heard that his regiment had been cut down on the battlefield, we all despaired of ever seeing him again. However, I recently got word that Robert is alive! Thanks to merciful Providence, he was spared. Not only that, but he is to receive a commendation for "extreme bravery in battle." It is typical of him that he refused to come to Paris to receive his commendation but has decided to return immediately to Nottingham.

Therefore, it seems very likely that you will see him before his own loving cousins do. I hope you will tell him that we are thinking of him and praying for him, and thank him for his brave service.

Emma paused, wondering what to write next. Fiona looked over her shoulder. "Oh, and do tell her about going to the restaurant. Such a quaint idea! It was perfectly delightful, a private room with white linen tablecloths and silverware and everything, just as one might have at home."

"Yes, yes," Emma muttered. "I will mention the

restaurant."

"And the balls," Fiona added. "Tell her that we are going to Lord Castlereagh's ball."

Emma set down her quill and turned to look up at her sister. "Anything else?"

Fiona grinned at her. "No, I think that will do."

Emma wrote for a while longer, then sealed the letter with a flourish."It's so wonderful to be able to give good news to a friend now that the war is over."

Fiona nodded. "Now all there is left to do is to bind up the nation's wounds with parchment and ink."

3

Gilded mirrors reflected the sparkle of chandeliers and diamond necklaces. Candlelight glinted on the medals pinned to uniforms of Prussian gray, Austrian green and bright British scarlet. Bubbles of feminine laughter rose above the sparkling hum of conversation in the elegant Parisian salon.

Emma sighed as she surveyed the political wits and sages who had been invited to the home of her aunt, Madame Odile Scatha, to discuss the issues of the day. Although peace had been declared weeks earlier, the lively atmosphere was tinged with a hint of desperation. Smiles looked strained, as if the glittering company expected a hail of cannonballs to suddenly burst through the tall arched windows, heralding a return to hostilities. The presence of thousands of Allied soldiers encamped in and around Paris did nothing to soothe anyone's fears.

Aunt Odile rapped Emma sharply on the shoulder with her ivory fan. "*Ma petite,* you must smile. Go. Talk to somebody, and listen to what they say."

"Yes, *Tante.*" Emma curtsied and took a step toward the gathering.

"Wait. Let me look at you." Deftly the older woman tweaked the curls of Emma's classically inspired coiffure and brushed one hand down the gauzy bronze silk of her high-waisted gown. "There. I was right, this color looks well on you. Now, go and sit with ...hmm, with Monsieur Talleyrand. Look how he is so bored by our Lord Parkington. You must rescue him immediately."

The great French diplomat was dressed even more splendidly than he had been that morning along the banks of the Seine, in a mauve-colored satin topcoat and a frothy white lace cravat. His gold-headed ebony cane rested against his knee. Lord Parkington leaned toward him, talking and gesticulating. Talleyrand lounged back in a gilt-edged chair, his hooded eyes unblinking, immobile as a lizard on a rock.

"Bored? How can you tell? He never moves. Does he even breathe?" Emma muttered.

Aunt Odile rapped her with the fan again. "Behave yourself and do as I say."

Lord Digby Parkington was most likely making a nuisance of himself. A diplomatic attaché in Lord Castlereagh's retinue, the pale, soft-looking young man in his mid-twenties looked down on anyone who wasn't lucky enough to have been born an English man. Emma, who was English but not a man, found his air of superiority and condescension extremely trying, especially when he attempted to explain the political situation in Europe to her. She knew as much as he did—and possibly more, since she decoded every secret communiqué sent to her Papa. Lord Forgall was the Duke of Wellington's spymaster, and she was the spymaster's top code-breaker. But that was a well-guarded secret, and she must not let her feelings get the better of her. She squared her shoulders and strode forward to do her duty.

As she approached, Monsieur Talleyrand's thin lips stretched into a smile. "Ah. Miss Forgall, it is a pleasure to see you again."

Emma smiled back at him. "What news from the court of King Louis XVIII? Are the French people still celebrating his return to power?"

Charles-Maurice de Talleyrand-Périgord, recently named Prince Talleyrand (although he preferred to be addressed simply as Monsieur), was an aristocrat who had clung to power through bloody revolution and Napoleonic empire. Now he had slipped skillfully into the restored king's court. He shrugged and opened his mouth to speak.

Lord Parkington spoke first. "Of course the Royalists are celebrating, but there are many factions which oppose France's return to monarchy. Lord Castlereagh believes—and I think I am not wrong in saying that the British government believes—that the restoration of the Bourbon monarchy is the best, most stable option for France at this time."

Talleyrand's mouth snapped shut and he resumed his impersonation of a lizard.

Emma, alarmed at the suggestion that Britain intended to foist their choice of ruler on an unwilling French people, looked around to see if anyone else was listening to Parkington's revelations. "But we would never—"

Lord Parkington ignored her words and continued. "We know that Tsar Alexander doesn't like Louis, and would have rather put his brother, the Duc d'Orleans, on the throne. However, we believe Louis is the more manageable of the two."

At that moment, Fiona hurried up and tapped Lord Parkington's shoulder. "Sir, Madame Scatha would very much like to speak to you. Urgently."

Once Lord Parkington excused himself to attend to Madame Scatha, Fiona settled into his place on the sofa and brushed a blonde curl off her shoulder. She smiled impishly at them, the only hint she'd just conducted a rescue mission.

Wryly, Emma considered her younger sister. Fiona's complexion was creamy, her hair a soft honey gold and her eyes a gentle brown. Blessed with a sweet disposition that endeared her to everyone she met, Fiona was adept at handling all sorts of people. By contrast, Emma's hair was black from widow's peak to stiffly curled ringlets, her eyes vivid green, and her features strong and decided. Her father relied upon her expertise with codes and cyphers, not people. Madame Scatha should have sent Fiona to Monsieur Talleyrand's rescue in the first place.

"I hope you won't take Lord Parkington's opinions too seriously," Emma told Talleyrand earnestly. "I'm sure Britain certainly wouldn't wish to impose any government on France, that was against the wishes of the French people."

Talleyrand smiled and waved a dismissive hand. "Do not worry, *chérie*. I would not allow it."

He sounded so confident that Emma laughed. However, he was a master of political strategy. No doubt he could, single-handedly, prevent Britain from doing any such thing.

A commotion at the entrance to the salon caused all three of them to turn their heads. The crowd at the door to the salon parted to reveal a military gentleman. For a moment he stood in the doorway, the center of attention. His glossy black hair was cut à la Brutus, curling at his temples; his features were dark and handsome, and his scarlet coat fit his muscular but compact frame like a glove.

It was Captain Killian, the young soldier who had rushed onto the bridge that morning and refused to allow its destruction. Reckless, hot-headed, and determined to get his own way. And her father had sent him here to be trained by Madame Scatha as a spy.

A French dandy lounging against a nearby column saw the newcomer and dropped his quizzing-glass. "*Sacré bleu!* It is the devil," he swore.

"What on earth is he doing here?" muttered a dowager to her companion as Aunt Odile moved to greet him.

Emma had an unobstructed view of him as he placed his hand on his heart and bowed to the salon's hostess. He smiled and lifted her fingertips to his lips for a light kiss. Madame Scatha blinked, and her mouth dropped open in a speechless round "O".

"Look, *Tante* Odile has been swept off her feet," Fiona whispered. "Will wonders never cease."

He straightened up and smiled at the stunned woman. Then he gestured to his companion, a gangling, ginger-haired giant with shoulders so wide they looked ready to burst out of his own scarlet frock coat. The giant bowed to Madame Scatha, who nodded a welcome.

"Oh, my," sighed Fiona.

Emma shot her sister a startled glance, surprised by the rapturous look on her sweet round face. *No, Fiona. Don't fall for the Irish cavalry officer*. But the signs were unmistakable. Fiona's eyes were shining as she watched the new arrivals. With unconscious coquetry, Emma's little sister swept a curl of her honey-colored hair off white shoulders bared by the low neck of her ivory gown.

How could Fiona set her heart on a particular man, without ever having spoken to him? Emma would have to give her sister a stern talking-to. Luckily, Emma herself was in no danger. She did not give her heart easily or lightly. Her father said that she had the right attitude, since it was hardly necessary for her to love the man he chose for her to marry. But Emma knew her father would probably never make her marry anyone, since the work she did was too valuable to let her go.

Determined to bring Fiona down to earth, she leaned toward her sister. "Do you know who that gentleman is?"

Fiona shook her head. "No, I don't. But oh, my. Just look at him."

"I'm looking," Emma muttered. With his dark hair and sparkling eyes, he was undeniably handsome. "I'm definitely looking." But that was all she was going to do.

Captain Killian turned his head and looked in Emma's direction. Their gazes locked, held. Emma's heart gave a sudden lurch. An indefinable expression crossed his handsome features. His eyes were the darkest brown, almost black, and sparkling with energy and wit.

In that moment, everything seemed to fade away – the glittering crowd, her sister's anxious questions, Monsieur Talleyrand's thoughtful hum – until she was aware of nothing except his dark eyes and the promise of excitement that he offered in his gaze.

Emma caught her breath. It was him. He was here. She could only hope that he didn't remember her from this morning, when she had spoken out against him. But she knew of Captain Killian's history, and she knew exactly why he was the wrong man to seek out Madame Scatha's tutelage. The skills Madame taught were not for wild Irish rogues, but for sternly disciplined, studious and clever individuals. Emma herself was Scatha's star pupil.

"Emma? Emma!" Fiona's sharp tug on her hand broke the spell. "Lord Parkington is coming back!"

The next moment, Captain Killian was bowing to her as Lord Parkington stood behind her with his arms crossed.

"How do you do," Emma murmured, uncomfortably aware of Lord Parkington breathing down her neck.

Monsieur Talleyrand said, "The brave Captain served with the Inniskilling Dragoons, I believe."

"Huh. Inniskilling. An Irish regiment," Lord Parkington sneered.

"I am Irish," Emma snapped. Lord Parkington had never served in the military at all. Everyone knew that the Inniskilling Dragoons had battled bravely during the Battle of Waterloo.

Captain Killian smiled at Emma. "Delighted to make your acquaintance, Miss Forgall. This is my friend, Lieutenant

Ryan Leary."

The red-haired giant nodded to Emma and then glanced at Fiona. He cleared his throat nervously and ran a finger under his fashionable neckcloth.

"This is my sister, Miss Fiona Forgall," Emma said, feeling a little sorry for the lieutenant. Despite his height and his bright red hair, one hardly noticed him next to his friend Captain Killian.

Fiona, her eyes downcast, plucked a speck of dust from her dress and said nothing. The giant cleared his throat again.

To fill the awkward silence, Emma turned to Captain Killian. "Where in Ireland are you from?"

"From Macha's Brooch," he replied.

The phrase rang a familiar bell, but where had she heard of Macha's Brooch before? Emma searched her memory. Macha was an ancient Celtic goddess...Her instinct for solving puzzles whispered to her, *It's a riddle.*

Lord Parkington snorted. "Impossible. I've never heard of such a place."

Why wouldn't Lord Parkington go away? Just because Emma's father approved of him, that didn't give him permission to act like he was her keeper.

She ignored him and thought about the riddle. In Celtic legend, the goddess Macha used the point of her brooch-pin to scratch the boundaries of the city of Ulster into the ground, and made her just-vanquished enemies dig its fortifications for her.

Macha's Brooch meant Ulster.

"Ulster is a great distance from Paris," Emma replied casually. "Where did you stop along the way, when you traveled here?"

Captain Killian shrugged. "We stopped in the home of the man who herds the cattle on the plain of Tethra."

"The what?" demanded Lord Parkington. "What are you talking about?"

Another riddle. She was beginning to enjoy herself. Good thing she knew her myths – Tethra was an ancient guardian deity ruling over the waters, and the "plain of Tethra" was the sea. Therefore, the cattle of the sea were...fish. Captain Killian had stayed at the home of a fisherman.

She nodded wisely. "So your host was a fisherman. No

doubt you had excellent fish for dinner?"

He grinned at her. "Most excellent fish."

Emma's heart gave a little hop of excitement at having guessed correctly. She smiled back at him and asked, "And where did your travels take you then?"

"Simple enough," replied Captain Killian. "We went over the Great Secret of the men of Dea, down the Great Crime, across to the Land of the Red Dragon, to the Ford of Oxen, and then to Caer-Lud. Then on to Lutetia."

"What nonsense are you spouting?" Lord Parkington howled. "Surely you can't pretend that you understand him, Miss Forgall!"

Emma waved him away like an annoying insect. Puzzles were like sweetmeats to her. She knew the ancient place-names of Celtic mythology and Roman history so well that she was able to decipher his cryptic comments. Besides, Lord Parkington's purple-faced frustration offered her a great deal of satisfaction.

"So, down the Boyne, over the River Delvin, across the sea to Wales, and then through Oxford to London. And here you are in Lutetia—or, as we call it, Paris." What fun this was! It was so rare to find another person who enjoyed playing these little games. What if they became friends, and could test each other with riddles all the time?

"Yes. Now tell me about yourself," Captain Killian said, nodding.

Called back to Earth, Emma spread her hands helplessly. There really wasn't much she could say about herself. Her existence so far had been very sheltered. It had been a necessary precaution. A spymaster's daughter could be too easily used as an enemy's bargaining chip in some diplomatic chess game. As a result, she had traveled farther in books than she'd ever been allowed to in real life.

"There isn't much to tell." Inspired by his riddling conversation, Emma responded with riddles of her own. "I am like Tara, the seat of the High Kings. I am a fortress on a hill, a watcher that no one sees, an eel hiding in the water. Like any good daughter, I welcome all but let no one in. And like a fortress I am well-guarded and protected by my father's men."

Captain Killian raised his eyebrows politely, but she knew he couldn't have understood her full meaning. Although he might remember seeing her in Wellington's carriage this morning, he didn't know who she really was. Very few people indeed knew that she spent her days deciphering messages concerning the most carefully-guarded battle plans and strategies of the British nation. Soldiers, even heroic cavalry dragoons, simply carried out those plans, that were laid by men far above the mortal fray—men like her father.

"And do they guard you well, your father's men?"

"Yes indeed," Emma said. "My father knows how to take care of his own. He is both a scholar and a strategist, infinitely clever and infinitely dangerous. Stronger men than you have been defeated by him, and wiser ones than you have underestimated him."

"Ha ha! That's the truth," Lord Parkington sneered. "Run along now, fellow."

They ignored him, intent on their battle of wits.

Captain Killian grinned at Emma and crossed his arms over his chest. "Ah, but then, you don't know how strong I am. Or how wise."

Emma stroked her chin thoughtfully. "True enough. I've never heard of you at all."

He flung up one hand in a gesture of surrender. "A hit, a very palpable hit. Then let me remedy that omission. Those who do know me can tell you that I'm as strong as any man you care to name, as clever as anyone you can imagine, and those who underestimate me do so at their peril."

"Impressive," Emma acknowledged with a condescending nod, "for someone as young as you. But I'm sure you'll do better with a little practice."

Captain Killian gave a shout of laughter.

His friend, Lieutenant Leary, nudged him and murmured something about an appointment. Captain Killian turned to Emma one last time.

"Well, proud damsel, I trust you'll think better of me now. Perhaps you will honor me by taking notice of my progress hereafter."

Emma gave him a majestic nod. "I shall be interested to learn of your future accomplishments. Do bear in mind that I couldn't possibly marry anyone who isn't clever enough to outsmart my father."

She extended her hand, and he bowed over it most correctly. For a moment, as his head dipped low over her fingers, she thought he might kiss them, as he'd kissed Madame Scatha's hand. But he did not.

Instead, he retreated backward a few steps from her before whirling around and leading his big red-headed friend out of the salon.

The dowager who had spoken earlier commented loudly to her companion, "Now there's a rackety young rogue, or I'm a Spaniard."

4

Emma looked up at the gold-embroidered turquoise silk canopy of her bed at Madame Scatha's house. She had been awakened by a street vendor's cart trundling down the cobblestoned avenue outside the house, but she didn't feel groggy or resentful. Her eyes had popped open, and she found she was actually looking forward to the day.

What was special? What was going to happen on this day? She couldn't think of any exciting events planned—just the normal round of duties that occupied every day. Then she remembered. Last night, she'd met an interesting man.

It was difficult to say why he'd been so interesting. He'd been perfectly proper, but as they'd talked, a tiny bubble of delight had thrilled her, rising inside her like a bubble running up the side of a champagne glass. A friend. She'd made a friend.

Emma scrambled out of bed and into her lace-trimmed peignoir as Madame Scatha's lady's maid, Marie, came in to open the curtains. She hummed as Marie put up her hair and helped her into her simple day-dress.

"Marie?"

"Oui, mademoiselle?" replied the maid, who was only a few years younger than herself.

Emma hesitated. How could she put her feelings into words? "Do you have a beau? A young man who ... whose company you enjoy?"

The corners of Marie's mouth turned down in a moue of distaste. "*Non*, certainly not! Men, they are only trouble.

Bah, I do not waste my time with them. They are all bad, even the French men, but the Russians, they are the worst."

"Oh," Emma said, a bit deflated. Of course the soldiers who occupied the city would not appeal to a Parisian woman.

Marie finished arranging her dress with a sharp pat. "You listen, mademoiselle, for it is I who tell you to keep your distance from all men. *Soyez sage!*"

With that, Marie sailed out of the room. Emma followed thoughtfully. She'd only spoken to the Captain once, after all. There was no sense in getting too excited. If there was one thing her father had taught her, it had been patience.

Patience turned out to be Emma's most-needed quality at breakfast. Her father didn't always arrive so early at Madame Scatha's house to work, but this morning he was already at the table and in no good mood.

"No coffee? Disgraceful," Lord Forgall grumped. "Even the street vendors have coffee."

Madame Scatha sipped her morning chocolate. "Then go to them, by all means. I should be very surprised to learn that what they are selling is coffee, in fact. Everything is in short supply these days."

"Talleyrand has coffee," Lord Forgall waved his butter knife. "Somehow he never has a short supply of anything."

Emma slid into her usual seat at the table, smiling at her sister Fiona, who was quietly crumbling a bread roll. Emma hoped to avoid her father's notice, but she was without luck. Lord Forgall turned his bad mood to his dark-haired daughter. "There you are, finally. Did you decode those dispatches, as I asked you to?"

"Almost, Father, I—"

"Ah, too busy flirting like a hussy with Irish cavalry officers?"

Emma's spine straightened. "I did no such thing." But her heart sank. Her father hadn't been at the salon, but he already knew what happened. Her father was so cool and controlled around other people, so imperturbable, and yet his scalding anger burst out all too often when he was with his daughters. Emma believed that her father loved her and Fiona, but that had never stopped him from lashing out at them in private.

"Yes you did. You're not to waste your time like that. You

will never marry a dragoon, because they're of no use to me. You will do your duty, girl."

He always knew everything. And he ruined anything that didn't suit his own needs. She'd had one rare moment of enjoyment, and now he had taken all the joy away from her.

"I do my duty, Papa. When have I ever refused to do anything you asked?"

"You don't fool me. You're just waiting for a chance to disobey me, but you won't get one."

Fiona spoke up, her soft brown eyes filling with sympathetic tears. "I was there, Papa. Emma did nothing wrong. Why won't you leave her alone?"

"*Ma petite—*" Madame Scatha began.

"Quiet, you." Lord Forgall glared at his second daughter. "Your sister should teach you code-breaking and mathematics, instead of impudence toward your father. But you're too stupid to learn."

Fiona, weeping, rushed out of the room. Madame Scatha shook her head.

Emma clenched her hands in her lap, as if physically holding on to her self-control. She was proud of how steady her voice was. "That was unkind, Papa. You know Fiona tries hard to please you, but cryptography is not her skill."

He pointed his finger at her. "But it is your skill. Think, girl! You've been highly trained. There's not one female in all of Paris, or Britain for that matter, who knows as much spycraft as you do."

Emma blinked in astonishment. "Thank—"

"Because I trained you! And this is how you repay me, by encouraging the advances of some bone-headed Irishman. I didn't put so much work into you for you to run off and become some broodmare." He slammed his fist on the table. "And that's final. Where are the dispatches you're supposed to work on?"

"On your desk in the study." Emma bowed her head in horror, realizing her mistake. She had forgotten to move the documents to the special room in the house where all top secret communiqués were kept under lock and key.

"Not in the safe room?"

"No, in the study. Lord—"

"Damn and blast!" He jumped to his feet, his chair toppling over with a crash. "How dare you leave such documents lying about in the open? You know better than that, girl!"

Emma drew in a breath, shocked. "But Lord Parkington told me to put it—"

"Don't try to blame someone else for your mistakes! You do what I tell you and do it correctly!" His face was scarlet with rage. Secrecy and security were paramount in their work—lives hung in the balance. Carelessness could mean death.

Emma felt her own rage mounting. She stood up. "You have always told me to do as Lord Parkington said! He refused to let me into the safe room while he was working in there, so I wasn't able to decipher it then! He told me to put it in your study. And when I went to ask you, you said—"

"Don't tell me what I said, girl! You deliberately disobeyed my standing orders."

"You told me to do as Lord Parkington said!" Emma had tried to return the documents to the safe room, but Lord Parkington had physically blocked her from entering. If he was working on something she wasn't supposed to know about, he could very well have covered up or hidden whatever it was, long enough for her to put the dispatches in their proper place. But without even listening, her father had sided with his protégé Lord Parkington.

Sick to her stomach and not able to eat any more, Emma threw her napkin down on the table. "Blame Lord Parkington, and not me."

She swept out of the room before she could burst into tears.

5

As he stepped up to the front door of the elegant Parisian mansion, Killian wondered what Madame Scatha would be like. He'd only seen her from far away at her salon the night before. A slender, animated woman with sharp black eyes and dark hair, fashionably dressed in a high-waisted gown the color of old gold, Madame Scatha appeared to be one of those sophisticated and subtle Frenchwomen who hid their true intentions behind flowery words and elegant misdirection. No doubt she'd have the devil of a time teaching him this diplomacy business. Mind-reading, ambiguity, and paradox were not to his taste. He preferred the direct approach: Fight beside one's friends, and fight against one's enemies. But he had sworn to learn whatever she had to teach. He would learn to deal in shades of gray, not just black and white.

He raised the dolphin-shaped knocker and gave it a sharp rap.

Leary hovered at his shoulder. "Who are you supposed to be meeting, then?"

"Her name is Madame Scatha." Killian glanced up at his friend. "She is going to teach me a new way to deal with our enemies."

Leary's wide, freckled brow wrinkled in puzzlement. "She's a woman warrior?"

"This is a different kind of warfare, I'm thinking."

Killian presented his card to the pretty serving-maid at the door . With a gesture, she ushered both men into the same luxurious salon where they'd been the evening before. It looked bigger, without the crowd of sophisticated ladies and gentlemen lounging against the brocade upholstery or leaning on the marble mantel.

The maid bobbed a curtsy. "Please to wait here, *messieurs.*"

Killian paced from tall, airy windows to the graceful arch of the fireplace. He inspected the bookcase full of books bound in matching leather. Leary gingerly lowered his large frame into a spindly side chair, as if fearing it would break under his weight. Unable to sit still, Killian crossed to the other end of the room to admire a delicate table with cabriole legs. It was topped with an inkwell and a writing-quill, proclaiming it as a lady's writing-desk. But sadly there were no half-finished letters on it for Killian to gather clues from. If one were to become a spy, why not start right away? The minutes ticked by.

Clearly this salon could not be where the work of diplomacy was carried out. The room was designed for entertaining, and Killian had run out of ways to entertain himself. Leary, after a few uncomfortable moments perched on the chair, opted instead to stand with his feet planted wide apart and his arms crossed over his massive chest. Killian sighed and draped one thigh over the writing table, swinging one Hessian-booted foot as he waited for someone to appear.

The door opened. Killian straightened up.

"Oh!" uttered Miss Emma Forgall. She paused at the threshold. her green eyes wide with surprise and maybe a hint of distress. What was there about his presence that would cause her distress? He had enjoyed their clever conversation the evening before, and he thought she had too. In her green and white printed cotton day-dress with a brown woolen shawl draped casually over her shoulders, she looked just as pretty as she had in her evening gown.

He bowed and smiled. "Miss Forgall."

"I beg your pardon. Madame will be with you shortly." She began to back out.

Another figure appeared in the doorway behind her. "Who's there, Emma?"

"Never mind, Fiona. Visitors for Madame. We shall leave you gentlemen to wait—"

Fiona stood tiptoe to peer over her sister's shoulder. "Is that Lieutenant Leary? What a surprise."

She pushed past Emma into the salon and curtseyed to the big man, chattering animatedly all the while. Leary bowed, ducking his head with a bashful smile, and allowed himself to be seated beside her on the sofa.

Because her sister was there, Emma reluctantly moved farther into the salon. "So. We meet again, Captain."

This wasn't the enthusiastic reception that he had hoped for. Sure, and he knew he had the gift of gab, but today he'd been expecting to use his gift on an older lady. He felt woefully unprepared to charm this younger one.

"Miss Forgall," Killian managed. "I thought—well, of course I knew—but—"

Emma raised her eyebrows. "That Madame Scatha is my aunt? Papa usually stays with the Duke of Wellington, but he spends a great deal of time here as well."

Killian gave himself a mental shake. *Charm. Gift of gab.* "Sure, and that's welcome news. 'Tis a blessing the war is ended, but the city hasn't yet recovered from its devastation. Hardly a place for civilians. How do you ladies entertain yourselves, here in Paris?"

Emma shrugged. "Much as we would at home. The city is returning to life. There are still balls and musicales and the opera, all as you'd expect. My sister and I even go out horse riding, when we can."

At the mention of her sister, Emma's attention drifted toward the sofa, where Fiona and Leary were deep in conversation. Emma frowned, and Killian guessed that she wasn't entirely pleased to see the two of them together. He, on the other hand, was glad that Leary's good qualities (or at least, those of his qualities that a woman might consider to be good) were being so well-appreciated.

He moved to block her view of the pair. "If you and your sister would like to go riding, I would be honored to escort you. The Bois de Boulogne is a pleasant place for a canter. Perhaps one day you might join me."

Emma blinked and focused on him. "You ride for pleasure, Captain?"

He nodded. "Yes, naturally. I was raised around horses from a child. Oh, they were fine ones we raised. Hunters, mostly, but race horses as well. Ascot, Newmarket, Epsom –

Horses from my family's stables have run in all those races."

"Impressive." Emma raised her eyebrows. "Is a love of horses what led you to serve in the Inniskilling Dragoons? But I don't understand why you'd want to expose a horse you cared about to the dangers of war. Battles are between men, not horses."

Well. She had done some research on him already, if she knew that he had served in the dragoons. "Oh, aye, there's danger, but a trained war horse is just as eager to rise to the challenge as the rider. We are a team. When we are in battle, my own Lia Macha is like a part of me." At least Lia Macha was safe in her stall these days. The horror of war was past now. Suddenly, Killian didn't feel like talking about war. "But when I'm not fighting, it's horse racing that I enjoy."

The conversation on the sofa had fallen silent, and his voice rang through the air of the salon. Fiona and Leary exchanged glances. Drawing a deep breath, Fiona asked Leary, "Do you ride racehorses too, sir?"

The red-haired giant laughed. "Me, miss? No, not hardly! I can handle the ribbons on any carriage you name. But I'm not a jockey, no."

Killian's heart was warmed by his friend's easy laugh. Leary was far too shy around women. Then he caught the narrowing of Emma's green eyes as she watched her sister, as if she was trying to decide whether to separate the two on the sofa.

To draw Emma's attention away from the couple, Killian struck a pose and sighed reminiscently. "Aye, racing is what I like. There's nothing better than a fine filly running her heart out and leaving the rest of the field in the dust. I like to see her flying her colors."

It worked. Emma caught the double-entendre in his words and gave him a level stare. "Speaking of the races," she drawled, "I enjoy a small flutter on the horses too. But I am very particular about the horses I wager on."

He grinned and leaned toward her. "Do tell. And what type of, ah, mounts pique your interest?"

"Hard to say. I prefer to watch them work out a little first, to see if they are front runners or come from behind. I like to know what their track record is, and learn what makes them run." Her expression was bland, but her green eyes sparkled. "I rather suspect you are as particular in your choices as I am."

Now they were no longer speaking about horses. "So you think you've sussed me out, do you?"

She looked him over. "I'd say you don't like to be judged according to the standard rating. You like to get out in front, open up a lead, take a little breather in the backstretch, and come home free."

He lifted an eyebrow. "You're no novice when it comes to horse racing, I see. But I'll be guessing you don't like to be prejudged yourself."

"I haven't met anyone yet who could do it," she retorted. "Do you think you could?"

Careful, now. This entire conversation was skating very close to outright impropriety. And she was the daughter of England's top spymaster—not a damsel to be trifled with. Still, a little bit of trifling never hurt anyone. "Well, I can't be certain until I've seen you over a distance of ground. You have the potential but..." He pursed his lips. "I don't know, how far you can go?"

"That depends on who's on the saddle."

Well, that was matching his bid and raising it. She was enjoying herself, or he was sorely mistaken.

She smirked. "I like the way you work. In case you don't know it, your judgment has been sound."

That was heartening. Nevertheless, it wouldn't do for him to assume that she was serious. Who knew, perhaps being in Paris had given her a taste for saucy badinage. He assumed a puzzled frown. "There's one thing I can't figure out."

"What makes me run?" She smiled.

He nodded.

Her upper lip curled into a delicate little sneer. "I'll give you a little hint. Sugar won't work. It's been tried."

Ah, well now. No sugar, is it? All of this risqué banter was just so much posing on her part. She'd flirted with him, but now she was warning him off. Perhaps this was one of those subtle little games that spies and diplomats played.

"So why are you trying to sweeten me up?" he asked bluntly. "Is there something you want from me?"

She shook her head, looking away. "No, I have my own plans."

"Do you now?" There must be some reason why she was playing this elaborate game with him, but for the life of him he couldn't see what it was.

She shrugged. "Of course, I know they haven't worked so well up to now."

A touch of wistfulness had crept into her voice, and he wondered what it meant. Perhaps this was her way of trying him out, seeing what sort of man he was. In that case, he was happy to enlighten her. "Let me give you some of my track record. My foster-father, Connar, raised me to be more than a simple farmer. I was reared in his noble court, among chariot chiefs and heroes, jesters and Druids. I was taught by the poets and learned men of Ulster, and they shared with me all their finest manners and their intellectual gifts."

"I thought you attended Oxford," Emma commented. "Who are these chariot chiefs and druids and learned men?"

"My kinsmen. They taught me wisdom and right judgment, respect for nature, skill in battle, and poetry. They taught me to fight for the honor of all alike," Killian said. "Then at Oxford, I learned the knowledge prized by the British. What about you?"

Emma drew herself up proudly. "I was brought up to respect the ancient virtues and to honor lawful behavior. My father raised me to be the equal to a queen—stately and noble in bearing, skilled and clever in knowledge. There is nothing I cannot discover about a person, no code I cannot break."

He was impressed. "If we worked together, we could achieve anything. I can't name any woman with half your skills."

"Have you no wife already?" She was blushing, but still looked him right in the eyes.

"I have not, indeed."

She turned away from him abruptly, looking out the window. "My sister Fiona will be the first of us to be married. It's only right."

He wasn't sure quite what to make of that statement. It didn't sound like a refusal. She seemed almost sad. He stepped up behind her, not willing to give up on the fragile rapport they had built. Though they weren't touching, he was so close he could feel the warmth of her body. She was looking out the window onto the city street, but he was enjoying a nearer prospect. He studied the wispy dark curls of hair that lay against her neck, the shell-like curve of her ear, and the smooth curve of her cheek. She was lovely in every way. His gaze traced the low-cut neckline of her dress, admiring the way it exposed her white throat and the soft upper slopes of her breasts. He could see her pulse fluttering under the creamy skin, and the rise and fall of her chest with her breath.

"Truly, it is not with your sister, but with yourself, I have fallen in love," he whispered.

Fiona's anxious voice interrupted this charged moment. "Emma, what are you and Captain Killian discussing?"

Without averting his gaze, Killian answered. "I was just about to comment on the lovely view before me. I could write a poem to the fair hills and valleys of that plain."

Emma stiffened, and her breathing quickened. Just loud enough for Killian to hear, she said, "No one comes to this plain who does not earn the right by battling our enemies while preserving our friends."

Fiona stepped up to Emma's side, and Leary appeared on Killian's other side.

Leary bent his tall frame a bit and squinted out the window. "There are no hills and valleys out there, Killian old boy. That's a Paris street, that is."

"I shall battle the ones and save the others, to preserve and protect the fair hills and valleys," murmured Killian.

Fiona looked from her sister to Killian, a puzzled frown on her pretty face. "Are you thinking of France's landscape? Or perhaps you are referring to Ireland's hills and valleys?"

"No one comes to this plain," said Emma to Killian, "who is not skilled in battle, and also skilled at winning without a battle."

"Ah!" Leary nodded to Fiona. "The plain! They must be speaking of Waterloo. That was a fairly large field, which one might call a plain."

"Well, if you say so, Mr. Leary."

"I can fight and win, and I can win without fighting," said Killian.

"When you have won, I will accept your offer," Emma replied.

Fiona whispered, "What on earth are they talking about?"

"Who can tell," Leary responded. "Dicked in the nob, both of them."

The door opened behind them. "Monsieur Killian?"

Killian, startled from his contemplation of hills and valleys, quickly turned to face Madame Scatha. He bowed extravagantly, mustered up his best smile. "It's most definitely at your service I am, Madame."

She nodded. Her sharp black eyes considered him for a moment, then her gaze swept around the room. "I hope Fiona and Emma have kept you and your companion entertained? Come with me. Emma, Fiona, you will look after Lieutenant Leary."

He followed her into the adjoining room, a dark-paneled study with cabinets and bookcases lining the walls. Madame Scatha took a seat behind the huge walnut desk that filled the middle of the room. With a little tsk of disapproval, she slid a stack of papers from the desk's surface into a drawer. Killian stood facing her, not willing to sit in the tiny chair allotted to visitors.

Madame Scatha rang a little bell. "I shall order tea – or do you prefer whiskey, Captain?"

"No. Tea would be delightful," Killian said, tugging at his cravat. His collar-points had suddenly become too high and his neckcloth too tight for comfort.

She gave the order to the maid, then her attention turned to him. "So. Milord Forgall says you were a fierce fighter, who now wishes to serve the Duke as a diplomat. Is this so?"

"Yes, Madame."

"Then we shall see, what are you good at doing, and what not so good? Some people are good with numbers, some with words, some with other people. Me, I think you are good with other people. So we shall start there."

"As you wish, Madame."

"*Eh bien,* we shall start. Diplomacy is a species of war. Do you understand?"

The maid reappeared with a tea tray. After she'd gone away again, Killian answered cautiously, "How so, Madame?"

"You must know yourself, and you must know your opponent," Madame said, handing him his tea. "The first skill you need is that of observation of other people. So I shall set you a little test, to understand how good you are at observing that which happens around you. Do not worry, this is remarkably simple. You can do it standing on your head!"

"Sure, and I will if you say so," Killian replied jovially. "Standing on my head."

"The new King Louis will attend the opera tonight. I wish for you attend as well. You will sit in a particular seat in my opera-box, which will give you an excellent vantage-point. You may observe what the king does, without being noticed yourself."

Killian suddenly became aware that his jaw was hanging open in surprise, and he shut his mouth with a snap. "That's it? That's all? What do you expect will happen?"

"Who knows," Madame said. "One cannot say if anything will happen, but you will watch carefully and report back to me."

Killian huffed out a half-chuckle. "What if nothing happens?"

"Then you will report that to me." Madame Scatha got to her feet, and Killian followed suit. As an afterthought, she added, "You have already met my niece, Miss Emma Forgall."

Killian bowed in acknowledgement. "I have had that pleasure."

"And what do you think of her?"

Sensing danger, Killian took a deep breath. What did this woman want him to say? It wouldn't be hard to praise Emma, but it was difficult to tell how serious he ought to be. Well, this would be his opportunity to be subtle. He made a wide, sweeping gesture with one hand. "'Tis every bit a queenly beauty she is, shining like the sun in glory, wise and clever in her speech, and noble as a castle on a hill."

"*Ah, monsieur,*" Madam Scatha said mournfully, "I observe that your heart has been stolen away by our Emma. But you must know, her father protects her very fiercely. Especially because she is so clever and of such importance to his work. Her lovely sister Fiona, of course she will marry whomever her father says, but Emma – no and no, *monsieur*. She will serve her father, and I am afraid that will be all that occupies her life."

"Surely her father wouldn't forbid her to marry," Killian

said.

Madame Scatha shrugged as she walked around the desk and came to stand beside him. "Me, I only say what I see." She patted him on the shoulder. "Very well. You shall return here this evening to escort the two young ladies to the opera."

"To escort—"

"Yes, and you may ask Lieutenant Leary if he wishes to attend as well. You shall make the party, no?" She ushered him out of the study.

"Wait—but I thought—a party?"

"*Naturellement.* What better way to conceal your true objective?" Madame Scatha said. "Just be sure that you are sitting in the correct seat, so you can observe what I have asked you to observe."

6

A thrill of delight caught Emma by surprise. She was going to the opera. Escorted by Captain Killian, too, and her father couldn't even complain about it, because Madame Scatha had ordered it. Quickly, however, her natural caution took over. Captain Killian was a flirt and a rogue, and his attention might easily wander to a flashier female. And what was Emma, after all, but a quiet, numbers-obsessed young woman, whose greatest skill was hidden like the proverbial light under the bushel? Also, her father would never consent to her marrying anybody. The more influence a husband had over her, the less influence her father could exert. And she knew that Lord Forgall expected his wishes to come first. But it was a tempting thought.

So, she calculated, there was probably no more than a sixty percent chance that tonight's trip to the opera would be an unqualified pleasure for her. And the chance that tonight's trip would be the beginning of an enduring romance were certainly close to zero.

Madame had just ushered Captain Killian and his friend out the door. They had sworn to return promptly at eight o'clock to escort them to the opera. In the meantime, Emma would have time to decide what to wear, to increase the probability of pleasure in tonight's entertainment.

"Remember, *mes petites*, you are to observe how well our new friend the Captain observes the events of the evening. And then you will tell me." Madame had wrapped herself in a giant knitted brown shawl over her usual carelessly elegant daytime outfit.

"What events do you expect him to observe?" Fiona asked.

Madame shrugged. "Possibly nothing at all. It is his capacity to observe without interfering, that I wish to know."

"But you do think something will happen?" Emma persisted.

"No, no! At least, I hope not. But you understand that all Paris is a powder-keg these days. The ultra-Royalists are demanding that fat old King Louis assert his divine right to rule, while the constitutionalists wish him to rule as the English kings do, as a rational man ruled by a constitution. Meanwhile, the Tsar is planning to gobble up Poland, and Prussia is biting off chunks of French land, and the vultures fly in from every nation to pick at the fallen body of our nation."

"But they're not all going to be at the opera," Fiona protested.

"We shall see," Madame Scatha said.

Sophie the maid entered the room. "Milord Parkington is back, Madame. Shall he enter?"

Emma, Fiona and Madame exchanged astonished looks.

"Oh, no!" Emma whispered. "What does he want? Why can't he leave us alone?"

"He may have a message from Father," Fiona pointed out. "But it's more likely he's come to see Emma."

"I don't want to see him," Emma retorted, feeling mutinous. Her heart was set on going to the opera tonight with Captain Killian, and Lord Parkington was intruding on her day.

Madame patted the couch. "Very well, we shall try to avoid him. Emma, *viens ici*, lie down on the sofa. You must try to look faint."

"But—"

"No, do not argue."

Emma obeyed, sitting down on the sofa as instructed. In a trice, Madame stripped off her big brown shawl and draped it over her like a blanket. The shawl covered Emma from neck to toes, completely hiding her. Madame pushed her shoulders back so that she was reclining on the sofa. "There, that will have to do. Try to look pale."

Madame turned to Sophie. "You may admit Milord Parkington now."

The maid nodded and left.

Emma murmured out of the corner of her mouth, "What rotten luck! He had better not be too difficult, for I insist on going to the opera tonight."

"That one is only too difficult." Madame muttered, then jumped to her feet to greet their unwelcome guest. "Milord Parkington! How delightful to see you! And now here, you see, our *pauvre* Emma is only just now recovering."

Lord Parkington exclaimed in dismay at the sight of Emma lying on the couch. "What is wrong, my dear?"

Despite the fact that she was supposed to be faint, Emma sat up straight and glared at him. Remembering her role, she clapped one hand to her forehead and sank back. "You take too many liberties, sir!"

He looked down at her. "Forgive me. I hope you will soon recover."

"Thank you," she said as tragically as she could.

Lord Parkington crossed his arms. "This is quite unusual. You are a magnificent sailor, a hearty eater, and your father says you've never been sick in your life."

"I have the headache," Emma snapped.

Lord Parkington relaxed. "Well, I had hoped to take you out for ices. Your father, though an estimable man, makes you work too hard. Young ladies should have the opportunity to be frivolous and charming. And what better place than Paris to do that?"

"Thank you," Emma said wanly. So far, she hadn't accepted any of Lord Parkington's invitations. Perhaps if she put up with him once or twice, he would leave her alone. "But we have an engagement tonight."

"Tonight! What have you planned for tonight?"

Emma shot an agonized glance at Madame Scatha. "Well I am not sure I –"

Madame interrupted. "You cannot expect us to account to you for everything we do, Lord Parkington. What a scandal!"

"We're going to the opera," Fiona said. "With Mr. Leary and – oh, many other people."

"The opera! How nice," Lord Parkington said. "But this afternoon—"

"My headache—" Emma put in.

"Then I have just the thing to remedy your headache. We shall go to the Café des Mille Colonnes and get ices." Lord

Parkington looked triumphant. "Surely that will make you feel better."

"Oh! That sounds wonderful!" Fiona said, clapping her hands in delight. She stopped when she saw Emma glaring at her. "Well—"

"It would be a pity to deprive your sister of this pleasure, Miss Forgall," Lord Parkington chided her. "Surely you don't want to disappoint Miss Fiona."

Emma gave up.

Shortly afterward, Emma, Fiona and Madame Scatha were in Lord Parkington's carriage on their way to the Café des Mille Colonnes.

"These fellows are mostly foreigners," Lord Parkington said, gesturing toward the soldiers who filled the streets and camped in the open spaces. "Austrians, Russians, Italians, what have you. Our lads are bivouacked just outside the city, along with some of the Germans and Belgians. The Prussian army is to the southwest of the city."

"Hundreds of thousands of them," murmured Madame Scatha. She shuddered.

"Our lads are gentlemen, as you'd expect," Lord Parkington added. "King Louis himself congratulated the Duke of Wellington on how well behaved his troops had been when they entered Paris. It was our fellows who stopped the Prussians from going on a rampage, and pulling down the column in the Place de Vendôme. Destructive bas—ah, blighters."

"With all these different countries here, who exactly controls France?" Emma asked. "The French king doesn't seem to be recognized as the sole power in the country."

"We Allies are in power," Lord Parkington answered. "For now, anyway. Not that our work is appreciated. It will take time before these bally Frenchies understand that we're here to keep the peace until the rightful government is established."

In the Palais-Royale neighborhood, they entered the pleasant Café des Mille-Colonnes. The interior walls and columns of the café were covered with mirrors, and sparkling chandeliers hung from the ceiling so that the entire room blazed with light. Soldiers in a variety of uniforms stood at the bar or sat at café tables. Ladies in summery dresses and hats giggled together as they enjoyed their ices, and eyed the dapper French beaux who smiled at them and twirled their mustaches.

"That woman behind the bar serving the ices is known as *La Belle Limonadière*," Lord Parkington told Emma out loud, as if the woman standing a few feet away from him could not hear what he said about her. "The Prussians buzz around her like bees."

He ordered ices for them in ungrammatical French, and the Lovely Lemonade Lady served him without expression. Madame Scatha's apologies to the woman were profuse.

"It is well," replied *La Belle Limonadière*. "One must accept these misfortunes for the moment. But you would be doing France a service if you persuaded these English to remove their camps from the Champs-Élysées. It is a great offense."

"I will do my best," Madame Scatha said.

Oblivious to their conversation, Lord Parkington was lecturing Emma. "These bally French officers are everywhere. They wear plain clothes, but you can tell who they are. They've all got large mustachios, ferocious expressions, and a sullen, discontented air."

Emma looked around. "They have suffered so much. Despite the luxury of the surroundings and the lively atmosphere, the French people look like an enormous grieving family. Look at them -- three people out of every five are wearing mourning."

Madame Scatha gasped. "Oh, there is Madame Fleuri. You girls wait here for just one moment while I go speak to her." She darted over to a café table occupied by an older woman in a black dress. After kisses on both cheeks, they settled down into an animated conversation.

"May I finish your lemon ice?" Fiona called after Madame, who merely waved at her. Taking that for permission, Fiona slid the dish to her own place and began to sample the contents.

Lord Parkington smiled at Emma. "It's a good thing you're in Paris," he said. "Not safe, of course, with all these soldiers and foreigners and other riff-raff, but far more convenient."

Emma raised her eyebrows. "Convenient?"

"You know that I won't be a mere underling forever."

"I'm sure," she replied, wondering where he was going with this.

"So when the time comes, its good to know that you will be here, close to me," Lord Parkington explained. "I've always had a special feeling for you. But I know you deserve better than someone in my current position. But soon, very soon, my fortunes will improve. And when they do, I'm glad that you will not be too far away."

Emma put down her spoon. Doubtfully she asked, "How are your fortunes going to improve? When?"

"You'll know when it happens. Not going to speak out of turn." He smiled a tense, insincere smile.

Fiona licked the last bits of lemon ice off her spoon. "I'm going to ask Madame for another," she said, and got to her feet. She hadn't paid attention to a single word of Lord Parkington's strange speech.

Lord Parkington was about to continue, when Emma's attention was drawn to a pair of new arrivals to the Café.

"Oh, look, it is Captain Killian and Lieutenant Leary," she said, glad for an excuse not to have to be alone with Lord Parkington anymore. She waved, and caught Captain Killian's eye. He elbowed his friend and they both came forward. The Captain's greeting to Lord Parkington was somewhat on the cool side, but he sounded happy to see Emma again.

"Miss Forgall, I'm thinking you're a ray of sunshine, for you brighten up my day," the Captain said. "One of these fine mornings, I'm hoping you will work with me, and teach me some of the skills I'll be needing to know."

"Yes, of course, Captain, I'd be delighted," Emma said warmly.

"You don't need to bother Miss Forgall," Lord Parkington interjected. "Madame Scatha can instruct you in everything you need to know."

These hostilities might have continued if Fiona had not noticed the two men's arrival and danced over to them. "Lieutenant Leary, the lemon ices here are delicious. Have you tried them before?"

When he confessed that he had not, she declared, "Then

you must, immediately!" Taking the stunned Leary by the arm, she led him over to the Lovely Lemonade Lady for his treat.

Emma shook her head. "I hope she's not going to order another lemon ice."

"I have always believed that it was a mistake for Lord Forgall to indulge his daughters in this way," Lord Parkington was saying in his usual pompous tone.

Emma frowned at him. "By allowing us to eat ices at the Café des Mille-Colonnes? How absurd you are!"

"No, by allowing you," Lord Parkington looked around suspiciously and then lowered his voice. "By allowing you to dabble in important matters. It is really not appropriate."

"I am not dabbling," Emma replied, outraged. "My father considers my assistance to be valuable."

Lord Parkington waved his hand. "Yes, but you should not even know about such things. You understand me, Captain Killian."

"Not I," replied the Captain promptly. "Sure and Miss Forgall has blood, brains and beauty, and brings joy to her father's life like a good daughter should. Why wouldn't she help him in his work?"

"I see there are certain matters that I must explain to you," Lord Parkington said. "Emma, I hope you will excuse us for a few moments while I speak to the Captain in private."

At that moment, Fiona and Leary returned to the table. Both of them were carrying dishes of lemon ice. Fiona looked very pleased with herself.

"Oh, no, Fiona, you didn't!" Emma objected as they sat down.

"Don't be so dismal," Fiona replied. "It's not as if I eat ices every day."

"If you have any more, I promise you there's a better than seventy percent chance you will regret it later on. If you become ill from eating all those lemon ices, you will miss our trip to the opera tonight." Fiona ignored her, and Emma turned her attention to Lieutenant Leary, in whose large hands the small dish of lemon ice looked like a decoration for a dollhouse. He picked up the petite spoon that accompanied the dish and studied it with consternation.

"Lieutenant Leary, would you please explain to my sister why she shouldn't eat so many ices?"

He shook his head. "Wouldn't want to deny her anything that gave her pleasure."

Fiona bestowed a dazzling smile on him. "How lovely of you to say so."

"Well, just remember later on that I told you so." Emma looked around for Captain Killian. The famous mirrored walls and columns of the Café tricked the eye and made it difficult to tell the patrons from their reflections, but after some careful searching she picked him out. He was sitting in a small alcove near the back door, lounging back in his chair with his ankle propped on his opposite knee and his arms crossed over his chest, listening to Lord Parkington, who leaned forward over the little table that separated them. Lord Parkington seemed to be doing all the talking.

What could they be discussing? She had to know — somehow, it seemed very likely that it had to do with her. She liked Captain Killian, and it would be too bad if he decided to take Lord Parkington's side when it came to the issue of her cryptographic work for her father.

She looked around the café, hoping to come up with some plan to overhear what they were saying. Eavesdropping wasn't nice, and she never even considered doing such a thing unless it was absolutely necessary. Now, however, it was necessary.

Madame Scatha was sitting at a table near the two men. Perhaps if she joined the two ladies, she could look interested in their chatter — which was sure to be full of reminiscences about their shared past — while capturing the gist of the two men's conversation.

She stood up. "I'm going to sit with *Tante* Odile for a while," she told Fiona, referring to Madame Scatha as Aunt Odile, as they often did when at home. "Lieutenant, I hope you will look after Fiona."

Leary nodded gravely, as if he'd just been entrusted with a task of high importance. "I shall."

"And no more ices for you," she admonished Fiona, who smiled so sweetly at her that Emma knew that Fiona wasn't going to heed her words. But Emma couldn't worry about her, when there were other problems to listen for.

* * *

Emma settled herself in a wire-legged chair across from Aunt Odile and her childhood friend Madame Fleuri, and pushed the chair discreetly backward, as close to Captain Killian and Lord Parkington as she dared. Her hearing was very good, and luckily this corner of the café was relatively quiet.

As she'd noticed from across the room, Lord Parkington was doing most of the talking, his voice low and intense. "You know Castlereagh is not the right man for this job. The fellow is unstable. He's no orator, and he's not well liked. The French hate him for wanting to bring back the monarchs that Napoleon overthrew. Still others hate him for favoring the most authoritarian style of rulers in Europe. Not the best man to create a framework for lasting peace."

"He's the Foreign Secretary," Killian pointed out. "Who else would do the job?"

"Oh, there are people," Parkington said vaguely. "There are better men to deal with this situation. Especially with the problems presented by a certain person who acts as King Louis' Foreign Minister."

"What's wrong with Talleyrand?"Killian asked.

"Keep your voice down, man," Parkington said in a fierce undertone. "You don't know who might be listening."

Emma looked around the café, watching the patrons chatter, boast and flirt as the mirrored walls multiplied them into infinity. What on earth was Lord Parkington talking about?

"So are you saying that we—that certain elements on our side wish to remove the man in question?"

The man in question. Lord Parkington worked for Emma's father. Did he secretly oppose Lord Castlereagh, and if so, why? Her father had always been a loyal subject of the British crown, even though as a spy he worked in a moral gray zone – to say the least.

"Yes. Who really knows where his loyalties lie? He's an aristocrat by birth, yet he served the revolutionaries. When Napoleon came to power, he became Napoleon's top adviser. And now that Louis XVIII is on the throne, who is named as his Foreign Minister?" Parkington argued. "There's no trusting a man when he changes sides like that."

"I'd be thinking that a good spy should be able to tell you which way a man like that will jump."

Lord Parkington's voice dropped lower, making it even harder for Emma to hear. "But we don't what to be plagued with the man forever. Don't you see? That's what you're here for. That's why — certain people have brought you in to our organization."

"I'm afraid I don't see at all." An edge of pure ice had formed on Killian's voice.

"You're a dragoon, for pity's sake! Nature didn't create you to be a subtle, inconspicuous spy, and I doubt you have the mental resources to learn the trade. You're a rogue, a wild man, a blunt instrument."

The chair scraped against the floor as Killian stood up. "We're done here."

"No no, I beg your pardon. I didn't mean to insult you—just saying how I see things. You're a man of action, a warrior. You've been in battle and you've killed before."

"Are you suggesting—"

Lord Parkington laughed loudly and waved a hand. "No, no, nothing like that. But there are dangers all around, sir. You don't know the half of it."

"What dangers?"

Lord Parkington's voice dropped lower again. "There are elements in the government that believe Monsieur Talleyrand is, shall we say, an impediment to our treating France the way it deserves after so many years of war. The people of Europe have suffered, sir."

"I have experienced the suffering caused by war," Killian said dryly.

"Then you can understand that it is better to remove any impediments to the course of justice as we see it."

"And Talleyrand is an impediment that you're asking me to remove?"

"Yes."

Emma gasped, attracting Aunt Odile's attention. "What is it, *ma chérie*? Are you unwell?"

"No, *Tante*," Emma said quickly, straining to hear what Killian's response would be.

"Ah, she has had too many ices," said Madame Fleuri with a wise expression. "Young women always do."

By the time she turned her attention back to the conversation behind her, it was over. Captain Killian was on his feet, bowing to Lord Parkington. He strode over to

Lieutenant Leary, spoke briefly to him, and the two men left the café.

Fiona rejoined them. "I wish I could live on lemon ices, but perhaps it is time for us to go. What is the matter, Emma?"

"Nothing," Emma said. "Nothing at all."

7

Operas at the *Académie Impériale de Musique* were not exactly Killian's idea of a good evening's fun, because they involved dressing up in his officer's uniform with its high collar, nipped-in waist, and brand-new, highly polished boots. But on the plus side, he would be attending with Emma. And he did like a good show. Apparently, they would be showing the latest new play, Castor and Pollux. It would be his first task as a spy: to observe King Louis XVIII of France and report back to Madame Scatha. It didn't sound too difficult.

As they mounted the steps of 2 Rue Richelieu, Killian extended his arm and Emma placed her hand on his sleeve. She looked marvelous, delectable, in a white gown trimmed with silver thread embroidered in a Greek key pattern. On her dark curls she wore several nodding ostrich plumes. Her eyes sparkled and she looked as though she were about to have a wonderful time. He hoped at least some of her good mood was the result of his presence, but he couldn't be sure of that.

In fact, there was now a certain reserve in her manner toward him, that she hadn't displayed before. He wondered what had happened. He thought back over their previous conversations, and he couldn't see that he'd done anything to upset her.

"Now, remember your instructions," she whispered to him. "Just watch the King's box –"

He patted her hand. "I know. I won't forget."

She smiled at him brilliantly, not as she would to a man whose company she enjoyed, but as if he were a very clever pet. He smiled back at her, his lips tight. How hard could it be to just watch someone? He certainly could manage that. Soon, he would find out what had gone wrong with Emma.

But for tonight, he told himself, the trick was to maintain his composure. A spy must be at all times calm and in control of himself. No calling attention to oneself with raised voice, or threats to fight someone, no growls or menacing glares. Only gracious nods, quiet smiles, and murmured pleasantries. Not too hard, if everyone remained polite. He patted Emma's hand again.

In the lobby, elegant ladies waved their fans vigorously in the hot, crowded space while officers in foreign uniforms of every color swaggered about, oblivious to the irritated glares of French citizens. For a moment, Killian felt a twinge of sympathy for the natives of this land, who disliked the feeling of being overrun. However, other nations must have felt the same way, back in the days when Napoleon's star was on the rise. Well, the wheel of fortune turned, raising some and dashing others to the ground.

Emma's gloved hand tightened on his sleeve, and she pulled him toward a small cluster of people. The group parted to admit her and they began to chat animatedly. He responded to numerous introductions with brief inclinations of his head. *Calm. Cool. Collected.*

Emma glanced up at him. "Oh, Captain, please find our seats. I must speak to Lady Castlereagh for a moment."

Killian bowed. "As you wish."

After a brief farewell to the group, he made his way up into the boxes that had been assigned to them. He found an usher who directed him to Madame Scatha's box. Slipping a coin into the hand of the usher, he opened the door.

He stopped. The box was occupied. In addition to Leary and Fiona and the unavoidable Lord Parkington, there were others: two Prussian officers, one tall and haughty with pale blond hair, and the other shorter, with short brown hair slicked back against his head.

He frowned, and then quickly took in a deep breath. *Cool calm collected.* He attempted a smile. "You've made a mistake. This is our box."

The pale haired Prussian frowned back at him. The well-cut chin jutted forward. "It is you who have made the mistake, *mein Herr*. As I have explained to these other people, this box is ours, mine and my friends. Not yours."

Killian gripped the hilt of the decorative sword hanging at his side. "We have made no mistake. Leave this opera box immediately."

The pale fellow's gaze traveled to Killian's hand, fisted around his sword. He rose from his chair, proving himself tall enough to loom over Killian. "Are you threatening me? Do you dare to offer me insult in this public place?"

"Oh, Lieutenant Leary," Fiona uttered, looking alarmed. She put one hand on Leary's sleeve.

Leary patted her hand. "Easy now, lads. Sure and we can work this out between ourselves."

Stay in the shadows. Do not call attention to yourself. Slowly, deliberately, Killian loosened his grip on the sword. He forced a smile. "No of course not. I merely informing you that this is our box and not yours. Check with the usher."

"Check with him yourself," the fellow snapped back. The two locked eyes and stared at each other.

Rage welled up within Killian. Insufferable arrogance! He wouldn't call the usher now if his life depended on it. He had a mission to accomplish, and he couldn't carry it out with this arrogant Prussian's interfering presence.

Leary tried again. "We're allies, and that's the truth of it. There's room enough for all, so let's have an end to this nonsense."

"*Ja,*" said the other Prussian, nodding vigorously. "There are enough seats."

Ignoring their protests, Killian advanced into the small space, crowding the big blonde Prussian back.

The Prussian barked, "What are you doing?"

"Sitting down in my seat," Killian replied, dodging past him and sliding into the chair the Prussian had just vacated.

"That is my seat!"

Killian folded his arms across his chest. He shook his head.

"Get out!"

Killian shook his head again.

"Now, lads—" Leary began.

The Prussian grabbed Killian's arm, and began to haul him out of the small chair. Killian tried to keep himself in the seat, but the fellow pulled him off balance.

"Get your hands off me," Killian snarled, freeing himself and raising his fists. The Prussian doubled up his own fists.

The theater had become oddly quiet. Killian risked a quick glance away from his antagonist. A sea of astonished faces were turned toward the two of them in the box. *Damn.*

"Captain Killian, what on Earth is going on?"

Emma stood in the doorway, her face an expression of dismay. The Prussian dropped his fists and stared at her. Killian felt the heat of embarrassment rising up his neck and flushing across his cheeks. He was supposed to be quietly observing, not fighting like a schoolboy.

Behind Emma stood several more women, all as elegantly dressed as she was. One was a voluptuous, golden haired beauty in a nearly transparent pink gown. She wore a galaxy of diamonds that shone and winked, making it all the harder to tear one's gaze away from her ample charms. Behind her was a small, weaselly-looking woman with a dour, pinched expression.

The golden haired one spoke. "*Lieber Gott,* Walter, what is this? Are you fighting with this gentleman?"

The pale Prussian shook his head. "No, it is he who—"

"This is our box," Killian interjected. He wasn't to blame for this situation.

"I'm sure Madame Scatha would wish us to share her box with you, Baroness Olga," Emma said. "We certainly wouldn't want to ruin your lovely evening with Walter."

Baroness Olga shook her head. "No, no, Miss Forgall. We did not realize you would be wanting the box tonight. I insist you take it. Walter and I will find other seats."

"*Nein,* we should all stay," put in the second Prussian fellow, who was universally ignored.

The arrogant Prussian Walter was giving Emma a very close and approving inspection. Now Killian was annoyed as well as embarrassed. How dare this fellow ogle Miss Forgall? Killian wasn't going to stand for it. He ought to call the Prussian out.

The fellow smirked at Emma and twirled his gingery mustache. "Excellent. There is room enough for all of us, if we do not mind close quarters. And close quarters with lovely ladies is always a pleasure," he purred, his tongue practically hanging out of his mouth.

Well, two people could play that game.

"Surprised you wouldn't rather be alone with this beautiful lady." Killian ogled the blonde energetically. The Prussian Walter was displeased, but Baroness Olga preened appreciatively and stood up even straighter, so he could get a better look. The grim-looking little woman in a plain dark dress, who seemed to be some sort of companion to the voluptuous Russian, gave a disapproving cluck and laid a hand on Baroness Olga's bare arm. *"Meine Dame,"* she said in a hissing undertone.

"Of course Captain Killian is happy to share." Emma said tartly, flouncing over to a seat at the end of the box closest to the stage.

Baroness Olga returned Killian's ogling with interest. "Miss Forgall, you must introduce this dashing gentleman to me."

"Baroness Olga Palenska, may I present Captain Stephen Killian of the Inniskilling Dragoons," Emma said reluctantly.

"Wonderful! And Miss Emma Forgall, may I present Freiherr Walter von Hentzow," Baroness Olga replied with a casual wave in Walter's direction. The fellow clicked his heels and bowed sharply to Emma, who answered with a graceful little curtsey.

Killian resumed his seat. As Madame Scatha had predicted, he had an excellent view of the Royal Box, at the center of the first row of boxes. Baroness Olga slithered into the seat beside him, arranging herself so that their knees touched. He shifted politely, but she pressed closer and fluttered her eyelashes at him.

*"Gemütlich—*I mean, cozy, is it not?"

The Prussian sat down on Baroness Olga's other side. After one last glare at Killian, he oozed closer to Emma, giving her a smarmy and lascivious grin. Frustrated, Killian clenched his fists and looked away. He could only hope that she was not taken in by his wiles. Killian had already pegged him as a bad one, but Emma might not have enough worldly experience to see through von Hentzow's façade.

Killian glanced over toward the Royal Box, to see the grand bulk of France's newly-restored King Louis XVIII settling into his seat. The King's fleshy face was sallow and he mopped a lace-trimmed handkerchief over his brow before smiling and waving the handkerchief in gracious acceptance of the audience's applause.

Baroness Olga whispered, "Have you met this King Louis yet? I admit, he is fat and not at all healthy, but he is well-read and quite an entertaining conversationalist."

Killian raised an eyebrow to encourage her to go on.

"He has agreed to rule as a constitutional monarch, which his rival the Comte d'Artois simply abhors. But your Duke of Wellington supports Louis, so—" She spread her hands in a gesture of resignation.

The evening's entertainment began. The more dedicated audience members trickled back to their seats as the orchestra struck up the music for the opera's allegorical prologue, celebrating the end of the Polish war of succession. Venus, the goddess of love, joined with Minerva, the goddess of wisdom, to subdue Mars. Love triumphed over all. In the boxes, less attentive audience members continued to socialize or even play cards until they were hushed by other theater-goers.

As allegorical Love triumphed, Killian looked over at King Louis, called *"le Desiré"* (the Desired One). So this was the monarch supported by the Duke of Wellington. Politically, the Iron Duke had agreed with Louis' decision not to seek revenge on the revolutionaries who murdered his older brother Louis XVI. But personally, Wellington preferred the company of the more vigorous and active Comte d'Artois. Killian wondered what secrets could be discovered simply by observing someone across a crowded theater.

In the shadows beside the large, throne-like seat that held King Louis stood the shadowy figure of a lean, hatchet-faced man dressed in plain dark clothing. Although the King didn't turn his head to address the man, the royal lips moved and the man bowed from the neck in response.

Baroness Olga's voice broke into his observations. "—a *tragédie en musique*, in which Castor and Pollux are twins, but Castor is mortal while Pollux is immortal. Both brothers love the same woman, Princess Telaira."

Killian turned politely toward her. "Oh. The same woman?"

She leaned closer to him, gazing into his eyes. "It is the power of love."

"I see." He leaned away from her.

Baroness Olga smiled. "Princess Telaira loves only Castor,

the mortal twin. When he is killed in battle—"

Suddenly, the audience started singing along with the cast. Beside him, Baroness Olga was singing too, consulting her program for the lyrics praising the king's return. The King nodded and waved, spreading his arms out in a gesture of gratitude as the song reached its end. The man in the shadows had disappeared.

Applause crashed through the audience, followed by a moment of quiet anticipation before the main performance of the evening. During this silence, the door at the rear of the opera box banged open. "What was all that caterwauling? What'd I miss?"

The slurred words came from a tall, hulking man whose uniform proclaimed him to be a British Army officer and whose bloodshot eyes and unsteady stance confirmed that he was thoroughly drunk.

Miss Emma Forgall gasped. "Ernest!"

The drunken officer sat down heavily in the one empty chair. "'Lo, sis." He looked around at the group and nodded at Fiona. "Sisses. Both of em. Howd'ye do."

Walter von Hentzow looked down his nose at the newcomer. "You are drunk, sir. You are not fit to be in the company of ladies."

"Not ladies," said the officer with careful dignity. "Sisters. All 'cept that lady there."

Baroness Olga put her gloved hand to her mouth and tittered. "Oh, Major Forgall."

Emma looked ready to weep with frustration. "Hush! If you intend to stay here, you must be quiet."

"I'm quiet," Major Ernest Forgall protested. "Ver' quiet." But for a wonder, he did quiet down as the opera began.

On stage, the Princess Telaira refused in song to marry her beloved's immortal brother Pollux. Jupiter, king of the gods, sang that Castor could only return to life if Pollux took his place in the underworld. Pollux nobly agreed, and the rejected Phoebe trilled an aria about unrequited love and her desire to join her beloved Pollux in the underworld.

Baroness Olga gripped Killian's bicep. "Doesn't this story wring your heart? It's so sad."

"Beg pardon?" asked Killian, who had been watching the King's box for any new developments.

A loud snore startled them. Major Forgall had fallen

asleep. A chorus of "Shh!" and "Quiet!" sounded from neighboring boxes. Leary reached out and shook the Major roughly by the shoulder.

"Quiet, ye drunken *spalpeen*," Leary growled.

Still asleep, the Major gave loud grunt and flung his arms and legs out. Cries of dismay erupted as they all cringed back from the Major's flying limbs.

"Whisht, ye addlepate," Leary hissed at Major Forgall, keeping an iron grip on his shoulder. "What do you mean by coming here in such a state? Go home, fellow!"

"Oh!" gasped Baroness Olga, staring at her feet. Following her gaze, Killian saw a large square diamond sparkling on the floor between her satin slippers.

Killian bent down to retrieve the gem. "Is this your—Ow."

His head collided with something hard and he sat back, dazed. The opera swam around him, three layers of box seats filled with pale disks of faces swirled before him like confetti. Baroness Olga's face, eyes and mouth round with astonishment, faded in and out of view. He closed his eyes and pressed his hand to his head.

8

Emma cringed as Ernest twitched violently in his drunken slumber, lashing out and striking the other opera-goers beside him in the box. At their cries of annoyance and pain, she sank as low as she could in her seat. Why did he have to act this way?

The play had reached the point where Phoebe furiously orders the demons of the underworld to prevent Pollux, whom she loves despite his disdain for her, from taking his brother Castor's place among the dead. *Combattez, démons furieux!*

Bodies lurched against Emma's as they avoided Ernest's errant limbs, and a small black notebook landed on the floor in front of her with a slap of leather on wood. Emma bent forward to pick it up, and her head exploded with stars.

"Ow!" Captain Killian uttered, dropping back into his seat with one hand over his eyes. Emma sat back as well, feeling dizzy from her collision with the Captain's hard head. Gingerly she felt her forehead, blinked, and looked down at the book in her hand. It flopped open. Instead of paragraphs, she saw lists of Cyrillic letters and numbers. She paused and looked closer, leafing through a few pages.

Her breath caught in her throat.

Dancers and singers began their dramatic battle on the stage. Emma ignored the muffled grunts coming from the rear of the opera box. It always took others a few moments to settle down after one of Ernest's outbursts, and she wanted to concentrate on the curious contents of the book.

The numbers were matched with Russian letters. Different combinations of letters and numbers were listed on each page. This was a code book – its pages contained the keys to deciphering coded Russian messages.

A violent shove from behind loosened her grip on the book and it slipped out of her hands. She dove for it as it fell. As the calfskin cover eluded Emma's grasping fingers, Baroness Olga cried out. Distracted, Emma glanced away from the book and saw a large diamond sparkling between the Russian woman's satin slippers.

Emma gasped. The diamond was the size of a hen's egg, cut in a distinctive cushion style.

"That's never the Regent Diamond?" Fiona blurted out, craning to see over Emma. "That's part of the Crown Jewels of France."

"It's mine, I saw it first." Baroness Olga reached for the sparkler.

Ernest let out a rip-roaring snort, and his Hessian-booted foot shot forward. His toe connected with the diamond, sending it careening off the front of the opera box and back behind Olga's chair. The Russian woman swiveled around in an attempt to locate it. Fiona jumped to her feet and leaned over her chair after the same object.

Emma turned back to pick up the code book. It was gone. "Where—"

"Ach, ye *spalpeen*, find yerself a proper doss." Leary grabbed Ernest under the arm and hauled him to his feet. In the process, he knocked the blond Prussian officer out of his chair. Walter von Hentzow staggered, righted himself, and turned on Leary with a snarl.

"How dare you push that fellow on me?"

"What happened to it?" Emma said again. She got down on her hands and knees to search under the chairs. "Where did it go?"

Above her and oblivious to her search, Killian thrust himself between Leary and Walter. "If you're too big a fool to know an accident from a deliberate act—"

Emma glanced up at the forest of legs and boots around her. "Would you please move out of the way? You could be trampling on it!"

"You insult me, sir!" Walter spat at Killian, his hand laid aggressively on his sword hilt. "I demand satisfaction!"

Her unconscious brother's boot heels left tracks of polish on the wooden floor as Leary grabbed him under his armpits and manhandled him toward the opera-box door. Emma shook her head and inched toward the far corner of the box, where a glimpse of white pages indicated that a small black book had fallen unnoticed. Several pairs of masculine feet trod on one another, and one foot kicked the book across the floor. Away from her. "Oof! Demand whatever you want, but do it later. This fellow is heavy as a rock. Can't you lend a hand?"

Boot heels shifted as Ernest flailed again and Walter's Prussian boots took a step back. Suddenly Walter fell backwards over Baroness Olga, who was on her hands and knees looking between their feet for the big diamond. Beside her, Olga's grim little duenna was tugging at her arm and begging her to get up off the floor.

Leary dragged his drunken burden out the door of the opera box.

At the sight of Walter upended like a turtle on his back, Killian began to laugh. At that moment Emma lunged for the code book, and his laughter ended abruptly in a whoop as she collided with his legs. His arms windmilled as he strove to keep his balance. "Good grief, what are you doing down there, woman?"

As if in a nightmare, Emma saw Walter reach for the small black book just as she was pulled away from her prize by Captain Killian's large hand wrapped around her upper arm. A booted toe kicked the book away again.

"The book!" By the time Emma managed to shake herself free from Killian's grip, the book was gone. "Oh no!"

"The diamond!" Fiona stretched out her hand to Baroness Olga. "That is the property of France."

Baroness Olga rose to her feet, and the gem disappeared into her décolletage. "Not at all. A tribute from an admirer."

"He took it," Emma pointed an accusing finger at Walter, who was still struggling to right himself.

Killian hauled Walter to his feet. "Give it back. Return—uh —whatever you took."

Yanking his green officer's jacket back into place, Walter drew out a white handkerchief and slapped it across Killian's face. "I demand satisfaction."

Emma's gaze swept around the auditorium. On stage, the

dancers twirled and grimaced in the Demon Dance. The music was loud and the violins had reached a screeching wail sufficient to cover the commotion in the opera-box, but one demon-dancer had run into the wings and was talking and gesturing at them.

Killian drew his sword. "Here's your satisfaction. Come at me!"

Emma, Fiona and Baroness Olga all shrieked. *Shhhhs* abounded from the neighboring boxes.

"Why you—" Red faced, Walter drew his own sword with a steely slither.

"You can't fight in here," Emma protested.

The opera-box door opened again, and Leary came back in. "Whisht, ye addle-pates! Ye cannot fight in the opera!"

The clash of two swords contradicted his statement, and Walter and Killian fought. Killian parried Walter's blows. Both were evenly matched.

As Emma held up her hands in a futile attempt to stop the sword fight, sweet little Fiona threw herself at Baroness Olga, trying to scoop the diamond out of the Russian woman's bodice. The two women toppled to the floor of the box, Baroness Olga swearing like a fishwife as she pulled Fiona's hair.

At that moment, the theater manager and the troupe's strong man charged into the box. "*Messieurs, mesdames,* you must leave immediately."

Leary grabbed Killian, pulling him back just as Walter's sword slid into Killian's upper arm. Then the theater's strong man punched Walter out, and the Prussian fell to the floor unconscious.

Emma was still explaining that it was all a mistake as the theater manager and the strong man escorted her along with Killian, Leary, Olga and Fiona out of the opera.

"But what about Freiherr von Hentzow? I must go back to him," she pleaded. "Please. You must let me go."

"What is that fellow to you?" Killian growled.

Emma pressed her lips together and shook her head. Wasn't it just like a man to assume she cared about some person she'd only just met? The truth was, she had just missed her golden chance to search Walter's fallen body for the Russian codebook.

"He started it," Killian muttered as Emma helped him into the carriage. His arm was throbbing, and he was angry with himself over not having been able to resist the Prussian's challenge. But really, no man could have ignored such provocation. "Quiet as a mouse, I was. Quieter. Silent. I was minding my own business, blending in, like a silently amused observer of the parade of human folly—"

"You fought a duel at the opera. You drew your sword first, causing a commotion that got us ejected from the theater and disgraced us in front of the King of France." Emma twitched her elbow out of Killian's grasp and pulled her skirts close. She seemed angry at him. Well, of course it was too bad that she hadn't been able to watch the end of the opera, although he didn't mind, since it meant he didn't have Baroness Olga whispering the nonsensical plot in his ear. But surely she ought to realize that it wasn't his fault. There were other people who rightly bore some of the blame.

The carriage rocked as Leary climbed in and sat next to Fiona. "It wasn't my fault. All I did was to remove this fellow." He jerked his thumb at Ernest, who was propped in the carriage's corner snoring.

Fiona, who was anxiously bending over her troublesome brother Ernest, glanced over her shoulder. "He's hardly ever this bad. Emma, why would he do this now?"

Emma shook her head.

A silence fell over the carriage. Leary carefully helped Killian remove his gold-braided military jacket, now sporting a rip where von Hentzow's blade had pierced it. The wound in Killian's bicep was a long, shallow scratch. After cleaning it with some whiskey he produced from a flask, Leary produced a strip of bandage from his pocket and tied it around the injury.

Fiona asked, "Do you always carry bandages with you everywhere?"

"Aye," Leary said, grinning at her.

None of them were taking his injury seriously.

"It hurts," Killian said. "It hurts like a thousand devils with ten thousand flaming hot needles, stabbing me again and again, so it does."

Emma glared at him. "You fought a duel. In a box. At the opera."

He wished she wouldn't harp on it. He knew perfectly well what he'd done. To change the subject, Killian said, "Is your brother prone to drinking too much? Perhaps someone knew of his tendency and wished to cause trouble for you."

"No," Emma said shortly. "I don't know. But if you had controlled yourself and not allowed yourself to be provoked —"

"I tell you it wasn't my fault! That fellow von Hentzow was a troublemaker from the time he first squatted in the opera box that belonged to Madame Scatha. I was following her orders to sit in a certain seat and observe the... well, to see what I could see." Killian crossed his arms over his chest. "Von Hentzow was spoiling for a fight."

"But you failed to see what was going on under your own nose, in our very own box," Emma snapped.

"Oh, and what would that be?" Killian answered sarcastically.

"That someone in that box had a Russian code book," Emma said. "I saw it, I had it in my hands, but I lost it when you and Walter started fighting."

"What exactly is this Russian code book?' Killian asked.

"It's a kind of dictionary for coded messages, " Emma explained grudgingly. "On each page, certain numbers stand for certain letters. Each page is different. To send a message, the sender chooses a page and turns the words of the message into the corresponding numbers as listed on that page. Then the sender adds the word or symbol that appears at the top of the page, to tell the recipient which page in their matching code book holds the key."

"So not every coded message uses the same code," Killian said. "Interesting. That must make the codes very hard to break, since they're not always the same."

"Exactly," Emma said. "We cannot rely on past messages to crack the code. But the code book explains them all. Such information is treasure beyond calculation to anyone seeking to decipher the secret messages of a government."

"As long as the Russians—or whoever—doesn't know you have the codebook," pointed out Leary.

"But we don't have the codebook now," Emma said with a

glare at Killian. "I almost did, until someone interfered."

"I didn't 'interfere,' as you put it," Killian replied indignantly. His attention had been on more important things, like crazed Prussian officers trying the skewer him with their swords. "As you well know. So who has the codebook now?"

"Walter von Hentzow, I believe. He saw the codebook and recognized it. It's possible that he sat in our box deliberately to obtain possession of the code book."

"From a Russian?"

Emma nodded. "Baroness Olga is Russian."

"Rather unfair to blame her, simply because she's Russian."

"You never know," Emma said, giving him an especially angry look. "Even people you think you can trust, will make the most deplorable decisions."

"And someone—Baroness Olga—had the Regent diamond!" Fiona said excitedly. "I could never mistake that priceless gem. It's part of the French crown jewels. In fact, many people believe that it's a symbol of France herself. There's a superstition attached to it as well. The one who holds such a treasure is divinely ordained to rule this land."

"Pretty story, but nobody in his right mind would take that seriously," scoffed Leary.

"Right mind or not, some people do," Fiona asserted. "Ultra-royalists want King Louis XVIII to be an absolute monarch, rather than a leader constrained by a constitution. People love tales about mystical signs and portents, and the story of a jewel that proves a man's royal destiny is very compelling. If it got out that the Regent is such a gem and has fallen into the hands of the Russians, I'm sure the rumors will fly."

"What if somebody in that box was trying to trade a Russian codebook for the Regent diamond?" Emma suggested, her eyes lighting up.

"Why would they do that?" Killian countered. "In your version, losing the Regent diamond would hurt France and losing the codebook would hurt Russia—who would win in this exchange?"

They looked at each other, their enthusiasm dwindling.

"Well," Emma said finally. "Someone else, I suppose."

"Or maybe there were two separate exchanges going on,"

Fiona suggested.

The others shook their heads. "Too unlikely."

"But we know who ended up with the codebook," Emma said. "Walter has it."

And we know who has the Regent diamond," Fiona added. "That Baroness Olga person."

"Right. That's it then," Emma said with a decisive nod.

"What's it?"

"We must go after them."

Killian shook his head. "That's a terrible idea," he said, but his companions were too excited by their theories to heed his words. Giving up, he leaned back in his corner of the carriage, crossed his arms and tipped his bicorne hat low over his brow, and pretended to sleep.

9

Upon their return from the opera, Emma led them into Madame Scatha's parlor. Madame Scatha looked up, set her book aside, and came forward to greet them. "How was the opera, *mes petits?* What did you discover?"

"Oh, *Tante*, we must—"

Before Emma could share her crack-brained idea to go after the Prussian officer whom she thought had the codebook, Killian stepped in front of her and grabbed Madame's hands. "Madame, you have to talk her out of this."

"Don't listen to him, *Tante*," Emma said. "This is very important. I must visit Walter von Hentzow as soon as possible."

Madame 's puzzled gaze shifted from one to the other. "*Quoi?*"

"You're not to go anywhere near that fellow without me," Killian said firmly. "Madame, tell her."

"No. You will only try to fight with him," Emma complained. "I want to find out if he has the codebook."

Madame flung up her hands in exasperation. "*Mon Dieu,* you are breaking my ears! What is going on?"

An involved explanation tumbled out of the group, with randomly added elaborations and modifications. Killian tried to make himself heard, but it was impossible. Madame frowned and switched her gaze from one to the other, looking more bewildered than ever.

"And I am certain Walter has the codebook," Emma finished.

Madame shook her head, as if trying to agitate the ideas in her mind until they settled into some sort of order.

"You said you weren't sure," Killian protested.

"Who else could it have been?"

"And we must find out from the French if the Regent diamond is missing from the Crown Jewels," Fiona added.

"Surely Monsieur Talleyrand could tell us that," Emma said. "The problem of the diamond can wait. The codebook is of vital importance."

Leary wagged his head slowly from side to side. "I'll be thinking it's pure nonsense, this plan of yours. It'll never work. How can a young lady search the house of a Prussian officer? Ye'll have to be asking someone to go with you, for a lady doesn't call on a gentleman, not even in Paris."

Emma stamped her foot in frustration. "I don't need any help. I don't want anyone to go with me. I shall—I shall think of a way. There is no time to waste."

Madame Scatha put her arms around Emma, hugging her and stroking her hair, as she might soothe an agitated toddler. "*Oh, ma pauvre petite!* Yes, yes, no doubt it is very important. No one can do it better than you, *hein*? And you are so ready for these excitements now, after spending all your days closeted in a room with your mathematics and your codes! Why not go to visit Monsieur Talleyrand first, and see if you can find out the whereabouts of the Regent diamond while you come up with a plan for tackling this so-dangerous Prussian? Baroness Olga often goes to Talleyrand's dinner parties."

Madame was overdoing it a bit with Emma. Killian had seen green recruits behave just like Emma when they got their first taste of excitement, but there was no need to treat her like an infant. If there was such a code book—and Emma was the person who would recognize such a thing—then it was an important prize. But letting her run off to von Hentzow's house by herself, without a plan, was also a terrible idea. He, Killian, would be much better suited to the job of breaking into another man's house and searching for valuable items. He just wished he knew what the code book looked like.

"In any event it is too late now," Madame added sensibly. "Rest, and tomorrow we shall make our plans."

Killian said, "Shall we return in the morning, and

accompany you over to visit Monsieur Talleyrand?"

Madam ushered Killian and Leary out the door. "You shall go first, to Monsieur Talleyrand's *levee*, and they will join you there later. Good night."

After the two men had left, Aunt Odile took Emma by the hand and led her over to the sofa. "Come, *petite,* sit down with me and tell me what is wrong." She patted the cushion beside her invitingly.

Emma shook her head. Leave it to her aunt to notice whenever something was amiss. So much had happened, but Emma couldn't help worrying about the conversation she had overheard in the café. What elements in the government had Lord Parkington been speaking of? And what plans were being cooked up, seemingly behind the backs of Lord Castlereagh and others? More importantly, what did her father know about all of it?

"I want to sit down with you, too," Fiona said. "But there's nothing wrong with me."

"Fiona, you sit over there, so quiet like a mouse, and Emma shall sit beside me," Aunt Odile said. Fiona sighed deeply and flung herself into the chair that had been assigned to her. "Emma, sit."

Sooner or later, Aunt Odile got her way, so she might as well do as she was asked. Emma sat down, crossing her arms over her chest and scowling. "There is nothing wrong with me."

"But yes there is," her aunt said. "You were acting so strangely at the café, and now you are still angry. What has happened?"

"Maybe Emma had too many ices," Fiona said, and stuck out her tongue. Her sister could be such a child sometimes, always wanting to be the center of attention.

"*Tschut! Tais-toi!*" Aunt Odile ordered and fixed her attention on Emma.

Emma flung up her hands. "Oh, all right. I did overhear something today in the café."

"What was it?"

Jumping to her feet, Emma paced back and forth. "*Tante,*

why did my father allow Captain Killian to come to you? Was it so that he could learn to be a spy, or—or was it for some other purpose?"

"What other purpose?"

Emma flung herself back onto the sofa beside her aunt. "I don't know. That is, I'm not sure. I didn't hear everything they said."

The truth was, she wouldn't put it past her father to coldly make use of a person's abilities even if it would bring harm to the one being used. Lord Forgall was a player on the world stage, and everyone around him had been selected for their usefulness in his pursuit of his strategic goals. It simply was too hard a truth for her to admit.

"Are you thinking of Captain Killian? He is an attractive man, *chérie*. He has that *élan,* that bold spirit, that lets him leap toward danger with a brave heart. And he is a bit of a rogue. But that is exactly why you must be cautious—he is brave, and he relies on his strength and bravery to survive. So he trusts too quickly, and it is a dangerous thing to trust an old spider like Milord Forgall."

Fiona sat bolt upright. "Papa is not an old spider!"

Aunt Odile shrugged. "Your papa is a wise man, but a dangerous one. He sits in the center of a web of information. It is like a spider to me."

"What about young spiders?" Emma mumbled.

"Ah, those you must guard yourself against with all your might," Aunt Odile advised. "Young men who are intriguers are very dangerous, indeed."

Fiona got to her feet and came to stand in front of Emma. She fitted her hands to her waist and glared down at her older sister. "So what have you been saying?"

"Nothing. I don't know."

Fiona snorted and tossed her honey-gold head. "I saw the Captain speaking to Lord Parkington this afternoon. All I can tell you is, if Captain Killian believes a word he says, then he's a fool. I don't know why Papa puts up with that awful Parkington."

"Nor do I," Emma agreed."But do you think Papa would want Captain Killian around, not because he thought the Captain could learn a new skill, but because he wanted him to fight and - and make trouble in some way?"

Once the words were out, Emma felt exhausted. It hadn't

been the whole truth, but it was as close as she could get to speaking her true fear out loud.

Aunt Odile and Fiona were silent for a moment, as they thought over her words. Finally, Fiona said, "Well, who knows what Papa is really thinking. But anyone would have to be a fool not to understand that working for Wellington's spymaster is not a safe sort of employment. And Lieutenant Leary says that his friend is not a fool."

As they walked down the quiet Parisian street, Killian said to Leary, "Do you think that the Prussian has the codebook? I wouldn't put it past him, the blackguard."

The rooms in which they had been billeted were above a small shop. The streets were deserted because the Allied generals had imposed a strict curfew on everyone living within the city of Paris. It was for the protection of the citizens, the Generals argued, because soldiers allowed to roam free were well known to cause trouble.

At the door of their quarters, Killian stopped and looked around. He motioned for Leary to continue upstairs.

"You go on," Killian told Leary. "I just want to see something."

Leary hesitated, frowned. "What? There's no one around."

Killian shook his head. He'd had a nagging sensation, a feeling as if he'd been followed. He looked down the narrow cobblestone street. The half-timbered upper storeys of the surrounding houses projected farther into the lane than their ground floors, turning the street into a small dark canyon. There was no one there. But still, he felt the need to double back and make sure.

"Just go. It's all right."

With a shrug, Leary tromped up the stairs.

Killian waited, one hand resting on the door but facing outward, scanning the street. It was dark and quiet. Had he been wrong?

Suddenly, a rush of footsteps alerted him that someone was coming. Running toward him. He whipped his sword out of its scabbard. "Halt!"

Into the lantern light that hung over the door of their hotel came the glint of gold braid. The light also sparked on the golden hair of the man who stopped, panting, in front of him. It was von Hentzow. The Prussian's sword was naked and his pale eyes were filled with the light of battle.

"Now you have no one to protect you." The Prussian charged him, sword slashing at Killian.

Killian parried the blow. "So is this the Prussian notion of a duel? Of honor? An attack on an unprepared opponent at midnight? You're no gentleman, you're a footpad!"

The Prussian roared wordlessly and attacked again. He was taller and heavier than Killian, and though Killian was no mean swordsman, the Prussian's relentless onslaught was daunting. Killian's earlier wound on the bicep of his sword arm was beginning to ache. It would only be a matter of time before the bigger man's pounding, hacking blows would wear Killian out. There had to be some way to end this.

"You sneak! You spy! What do you know of honor?" The Prussian bellowed between blows.

"Faith, you're the very devil of a madman," Killian said. "You began all this foolishness. What's the matter with you?"

Killian was so busy fending off the Prussian's enraged attack that he didn't think to call for Leary's help. He could feel himself weakening as he hunted for an opening in von Hentzow's style that would allow him to disable the fellow sand end the fight with the least harm possible.

Then, out of the corner of his eye, he saw two more Prussian soldiers materialize out of the darkness. They were officers, too, from the looks of them, with their gold-braided jackets and short capes swinging jauntily from their shoulders. Behind the soldiers were two thuggish Frenchmen. One of the thugs slapped a stout cudgel against his palm.

"Oh, this has gone far enough," Killian muttered. Gathering the last of his strength, he slashed through the Prussian's jacket sleeve. Blood seeped from von Hentzow's right arm and he roared in pain. Killian fell back, gasping.

The others advanced upon Killian. Both soldiers drew their swords and slashed at him at the same time. Killian dodged, sweeping his own sword around in a semicircle. The Prussians separated and attacked from opposite sides. The one on the left came too close and Killian grabbed the hem of his short uniform cape. Giving it a hard yank, he spun the fellow around. The soldier lost his footing and crashed into one of the thugs standing behind.

"Lucky that was my one good hand," Killian muttered. By now his sword arm was almost too weak to hold the weapon.

He slashed at the other soldier and then planted his foot square in the soldier's chest. With a might shove, he pushed him back. Then stood panting as the two thugs rushed forward. The one with the cudgel landed a sharp blow on Killian's shoulder.

Killian went down to one knee.

"Finish him!" Von Hentzow screamed to his henchmen.

Light spilled out into the street as the door to the hotel opened. Leary's voice said, "Now what's all this then?"

Fending off the second thug with a sweep of his blade, Killian growled, "I could use a hand."

Leary said, "Right you are." And he disappeared back into the house.

"Now!" Killian shouted desperately.

The thug with the cudgel attacked again. His thick club broke Killian's sword. "Ah, the devil fly away with you, you miserable cur," Killian snarled as he looked at the broken end in his hand. He swayed, staggered and widened his stance to hold himself up.

A whistle sounded at the end of the street, and some French policeman charged forward. "*Arretez-vous!*"

The French thugs vanished as if by magic, melting into the dark. The two Prussian soldiers lifted von Hentzau, who was clutching his wounded arm and groaning.

"This British fellow attacked me," von Hentzow claimed dramatically. His French was perfect and very fluent. "See how he has injured me. I may never be able to use my arm again."

The French policeman glared at Killian, who had staggered over to lean against the wall. Killian shook his head and waved his broken sword.

Leary reemerged with his sword drawn. Taking in the scene, with the Prussian soldiers holding von Hentzow and the gendarme standing before him with pad and pencil poised, he lowered its point and relaxed. "Oh good. The police are here to remove these Prussian fellows."

The French policeman stalked over to Killian and barked,

"Why are you disturbing the peace and attacking these soldiers?"

"They attacked me!" Killian protested wearily as he leaned against the wall, exhausted.

"But you have wounded this man, *monsieur*," the policeman said, pointing at the Prussian. "This is a very great crime."

"Arrest him," the Prussian demanded. "I am wounded, possibly injured for life."

Leary's jaw dropped open in amazement. The big redhead sneered, "And sure, isn't it himself who is crying to the Heavens to save him from the Irishman, for if you had forty Prussians with their swords drawn charging at you, 'twouldn't be no more than a fair fight."

"Don't be putting ideas into his head," Killian admonished him, and then turned to the gendarme. "It was the Prussian who started it. My friend and I were walking home like good Christians when we were attacked."

At the other end of the street, two more people appeared. An older gentleman, impeccably dressed from his powdered wig to his unblemished white stockings led the way. Killian's mouth dropped as he recognized the fine satin coat, the fantastically embroidered waistcoat, and the ebony cane that supported his limping walk. Mechlin lace dripped from his coat sleeves and in one hand he carried a snowy handkerchief. Peeking out from behind this impressive gentleman was the second person, a servant dressed in livery carrying a slate and some chalk.

The elegant gentleman raised his eyebrows and uttered a mild curse in French. "All these soldiers. What are they doing infesting my beautiful Paris? All France is in a sad state these days, is she not, my dear Le Hamand?"

"Yes Monseigneur," the valet murmured.

Killian watched as the French policemen turned and bowed to Monsieur Talleyrand. They murmured greetings and apologies, to which the gentleman listened patiently.

Finally, he nodded and addressed the Prussian. "My dear sir, if you wish to file charges, then this poor gendarme shall be forced to take you all down to the station to file a formal complaint. Surely this will take many hours and much writing to settle."

The Prussian said stubbornly, "He attacked me in an

unprovoked fashion, und he has wounded me grievously."

"I did nothing of the sort!" Killian retorted. "You and your henchmen followed us to our hotel to attack us."

At this, Talleyrand raised his eyebrows and exchanged a look with the gendarme. The policeman nodded.

Blowing out an exasperated breath, the gendarme turned to address Killian and the Prussian. "You foreign soldiers must keep these private quarrels to your selves. You are disturbing the peace. If you are discovered dueling in the streets again, I shall arrest you both and throw you into prison."

"And inform your superior officers," Talleyrand said softly.

"And I shall also inform your superior officers," the policeman added.

Talleyrand shook the lace on his cuffs and plucked an invisible speck of lint off his sleeve. "I think that is all. Good night, gentlemen."

Without any further ado, the elegant Foreign Minister proceeded along his limping way with his valet, Le Hamand, scurrying after him. The gendarme cleared his throat, slapped his notebook shut, and bowed before turning smartly on his heel and marching away.

Von Hentzow glared at Talleyrand's retreating back. Then he turned and snarled wordlessly at Killian before allowing his companions to carry him away.

Leary took Killian by his uninjured arm. "Now, wasn't that a holy show of a fight. What do you mean by letting the fellow have a second bite at you?"

"Sure, and you don't think I let him, do you?" Killian replied. "He waylaid us."

"And who might that fine French fellow have been?"

"That, my old horse, was none other than Monsieur Talleyrand, the French Foreign Minister."

Leary cast a suspicious look down the street in the direction that Talleyrand had taken. "Well, minister or no, he's a right *sleeveen* with a face on him like a bag of spuds."

Killian sighed. "*Sleeveen*, you say? Sure and he's a smooth devil, but tonight I was very grateful for his help."

Drawing him into the house, Leary shut the door behind them and hustled him upstairs. "Let me look at your shoulder. Ye took a mighty blow. We'll have to get you a new sword, too."

"Emma Forgall wants to search the Prussian's house, God pardon her for rushing in where angels should fear to tread."

"And you're thinking to go with her? I would like to see his face when you're standing on his doorstep, smiling like butter wouldn't melt in your mouth," Leary said. "He'd never let you in, no more than if you were offering him those Crown Jewels."

"There will be another way. We just have to find it."

"Good luck with that," Leary said glumly.

10

"But Emma, why must we go now?" Fiona complained as she hurried to the carriage in Emma's wake. "Monsieur Talleyrand is barely awake at this time of day."

"Nonsense, it's after noon," Emma flung over her shoulder. She had waited all morning. After last night's fight at the opera, and the code book, and the diamond, she needed to speak with Monsieur Talleyrand. Oh, she didn't intend tell him everything that had happened (especially not about the code book) but he was the one person who would be likely to know what plots and intrigues were going on in Paris. A little delicate probing would suffice, especially if she got to him early, before the chaotic scene at the opera became common knowledge.

"He doesn't wake up until noon," Fiona said. "And he's not even presentable until at least one in the afternoon. Dorothea told me so."

"Men often go to visit him earlier than this." Emma climbed into the carriage.

Fiona followed her. "Yes, but they don't mind seeing him in his underwear."

It was a short carriage ride to Talleyrand's residence on the Place de la Concorde. Fiona fanned herself, adding her own efforts to the faint breeze that did little to lift the summertime heat. Together they climbed the stairs into the minister's house.

As Fiona had said, the minister was not at home to ladies just yet. Emma reluctantly conceded that her sister had been right, and they settled in a small, elegant parlor to wait. To Emma's surprise, Killian walked in and greeted them.

"Captain! What brings you here?"

Killian sat down stiffly, with a barely concealed grimace. "I've some questions to ask the minister. He's got some other people in there whispering into his ear, so I thought I'd wait."

Fiona leaned forward and asked eagerly, "What does he do in there? All the gentlemen roll their eyes and make such faces about it and I tried to ask Papa to explain, but he would not."

"Fiona!" Emma remonstrated, scandalized.

Killian laughed. "Your father is right. Sure and the minister's a fine fellow, but a man's morning routine is best left to himself. Oh." He grimaced and put a hand on his shoulder.

Emma frowned at Killian. "Why are you groaning like that? What happened to you?"

Leary entered the parlor and Fiona ran to meet him. "Lieutenant Leary!" She stopped suddenly a few feet away from him, hung her head and twisted her hands together. "How do you do?"

"Fine, and your own lovely self?" Leary replied with a bashful smile. He looked away, but his pale skin turned a tell-tale red.

"Lieutenant Leary, what has happened to the Captain?" Emma demanded.

Leary shrugged. "Wasn't it that Prussian, then, and four of his lads who come by late last night, spoiling for a fight."

Fiona gasped and stared wide-eyed at Leary. "Freiherr von Hentzow fought with you and the Captain?"

"They all fought Killian," Leary corrected her. "T'were all over by the time I got me sword."

"Captain Killian, am I to understand that you singlehandedly fought off five attackers last night?" Emma demanded.

"One of them caught him a great belt on the shoulder," Leary reported.

Killian shook his head ruefully. "And wasn't it Monsieur Talleyrand who settled it all. The old gent came swaying up, said 'What's all this then,' and they all slunk back into their holes. So we came by this morning to thank him."

Emma focused her attention on Killian. "Were you badly hurt? Have you seen a doctor yet? I can provide you with some liniment if you like." She rose from her chair and came over to stand in front of Killian. She touched his shoulder delicately, with the tips of her fingers. "Is this where it hurts?"

Killian flinched and grabbed her fingers, holding them away. "No. It's all right."

The touch of his warm hand on hers sent a shock through her, and she froze. She looked up from his shoulder to his face, and their gazes locked. What she saw made her breath quicken and her heart pound. His eyes were the darkest brown, almost black, surrounded by the longest lashes she'd ever seen in a man. Dark curls fell in wild abandon over his wide brow, and his firm, well-cut lips were slightly parted, as if he were about to ask her a question. His gaze was serious, challenging even, very different from his normally merry expression.

"I'm sorry if I hurt you," she whispered, suddenly shaken by the unexpected connection she felt between them. She tried to pull back, but he didn't release her.

"You didn't," he said softly, his eyes still searching her face.

She huffed out a little laugh and smiled, breaking the connection. "I'm very glad. Please do let me know if there's anything I can do."

"Sure and I shall." He released her hand and smiled back.

Talleyrand entered the parlor then, dressed with his usual care. "*Mes amis*," he said jovially, "I regret that I have kept you waiting."

Fiona rushed into speech. "Oh, Monsieur Talleyrand, you'll never believe what happened at the opera."

Talleyrand drew back in mock astonishment at her sudden outpouring, then smiled indulgently. "*Oh là là!* You must tell me immediately."

The story about the large gem that looked just like the Regent Diamond tumbled out—How someone dropped it on the floor of the opera-box; how Fiona had vied with Baroness Olga for it; and how it had slipped through Fiona's hands like a bar of soap in the tub. Fiona made an entertaining story of it and Talleyrand had listened with evident pleasure. Emma was simply relieved that the tale had been told without any references to code books.

"So, what I wish to know is," Fiona concluded, "Do you know if the French King still has all the crown jewels?"

"I hope so," Talleyrand replied. "The Regent Diamond is a most significant jewel! It is the purest and most beautiful diamond in the world. It was set into the crown of Louis XV, and then of his successor Louis XIV, and Queen Marie Antoinette wore it in her hair. The jewel was stolen during the Revolution, and later Napoleon mounted it in the pommel of his sword. Now King Louis XVIII has arranged to have it mounted on his coronation crown as a symbol of the continuity of the Royal line."

"Considering what happened to Louis XIV, Marie Antoinette, and to Napoleon, one wonders if it's not bad luck," Killian commented. "Maybe the new king Louis ought to reconsider making use of it."

"No, no, it is too beautiful not to us," Fiona said. "Surely you don't believe such old wives' tales!"

"Thank you, Mademoiselle. I shall be sure to inquire after the Regent Diamond," Talleyrand assured Fiona, "To make sure the jewel has not gone missing."

Inspired by the minister's warm interest in the story about the Regent Diamond, Emma drew in a breath to ask her own questions. Then she hesitated. How could she find out what Talleyrand knew without giving away too much information?

Talleyrand tilted his head to one side and raised his eyebrows at her. "Yes?"

Cautiously, she asked, "Monsieur, do you know anything about how the Russians send secret messages to one another? I mean, about what kinds of codes they use?"

He shrugged dismissively. "My child, I do not pry, I merely listen when people tell me things. This business of prying I leave to others."

Emma felt heat rising in her cheeks. "Very sensible, I'm sure." An important minister like Talleyrand probably didn't bother with details like codes and ciphers.

"Monsieur, since you are so open to answering questions today, I've got one for you," Killian put in.

Talleyrand removed a gold pocket watch from his waistcoat pocket, flipped open the lid and checked the time. "Perhaps, if it is brief. I am desolated to inform you that I must hurry off to our daily cabinet meeting in just a few minutes."

"At the opera, there was a man who hid in the shadows beside King Louis and spoke to him," Killian said quickly. "He was dressed in plain dark clothes. A thin, pinched-looking man, with the ruthless air of a starving wolf."

"Ah. You are describing Fouché," Talleyrand murmurs. "He is the Minister of Police. Ruthless is just the word for him. He is quite ferocious, pursuing the enemies of whichever master holds his leash. Under Napoleon he terrorized the aristocracy; these days, I hear he's planning to arrest Marshal Ney, who fought so bravely at the battle of Waterloo. They say five horses were shot from under Ney. It was as if he sought death that day, but death did not want him. Now, perhaps, through Fouché, he will get his wish."

"This Fouché sounds like an evil man," Killian commented. "I wonder the King would speak with him."

"A necessary evil," Talleyrand replied. "And your Wellington agrees, since he has foisted Fouché upon me as the Minister of Police, to suppress any unrest that may occur. Bah!"

"So you do not find him necessary?"

"Fouché wants to punish as many people as he can, but I do not wish for any more blood. It is time to rebuild, to heal, to forgive."

"What will you do?"

Talleyrand checked his pocket watch again. "Oh, I shall think of something. Travel is so invigorating, don't you agree? I spent two years in America. Marvelous country. Magnificent forests, wide open spaces. The Potomac River is beautiful, unlike any river in Europe. Travel, it is good for the soul."

France's foreign minister and intriguer par excellence smiled at them all, gave them a quick nod and limped away down the hall.

Emma exchanged a glance with Killian. She lifted one eyebrow. "I predict that Joseph Fouché will soon embark upon a long sea voyage."

Later that day, Killian followed Emma into the small parlor

she usually used for work. Books were stacked on the round table in the center of the room. Reports bound with red tape were piled on the floor, and papers covered with jotted notes cascaded off a chair. A small clear spot on the table showed where Emma actually did her work. Hastily, Emma swept the notes off the chair and gestured for him to sit.

"It all has to be put away when I'm not here," she explained. "But while I'm working, I like to have them nearby."

He sat and watched her bustle around the room. She was still wary of him, but she appeared to have decided not to hold a grudge. One day, perhaps, he would ask her what had gone wrong.

"Now, here is some paper for you to write on, and there should be an inkwell somewhere." She hunted under several piles of paper before finding the inkwell. "And a quill. I have several quills."

Finally, she sat down beside him with a sigh of relief.

He smiled at her. He'd been nervous about this moment, his first lesson in cryptography, but seeing her so flustered gave him a little confidence. "Sure and I'm looking forward to our lesson. Any subject that is so fascinating to you will be a treat to learn."

Her expression was so doubtful that he almost laughed out loud. "Really? Well, I hope so." She shifted uncomfortably in her chair. "Not everyone finds it so fascinating."

Killian couldn't help saying, "I'm thinking Lord Parkington finds it fascinating, him being such a favorite of Lord Forgall's and all."

Now where did that come from? He wasn't jealous, not a bit of it, but the sad truth was that Lord high-and-mighty Parkington rubbed him the wrong way. Gave himself airs with all his sneering and posing, and him no better than an Englishman.

"Oh, no, not at all," Emma said distantly. He was gratified by her lack of interest in, even her dislike of, Lord Parkington. Just mentioning his name made her poker up. "He finds cryptography a terrible bore. Now, let's start with the basics."

Killian pulled his chair in closer to hers, enjoying the cozy feeling of sitting cheek to cheek. The light scent of her violet perfume tickled his nose. As she talked, he enjoyed the sound of her voice.

"In letter-for-letter substitution cyphers, a great deal depends on knowing how often any given letter is used in a particular language. For instance, the letter "e" is the most frequently-appearing letter in the English language. So in a message using the letter-substitution code, the letter that appears most frequently probably stands for "e". Do you see?" Emma was saying. "Now, according to Laplace's mathematical system of inductive reasoning based on probability—"

"Stop! My head is whirling," complained Killian.

Emma sat back and regarded him with mild astonishment. "Oh. Perhaps you have not yet read Count Laplace's Essay on Probabilities?"

"No," Killian said in a strangled voice.

"Well, it was only published last year," she said forgivingly.

"Maybe there is some other intelligence-gathering activity that you could teach me," Killian suggested. "Something with less math and more physical activity?"

Emma looked puzzled.

Killian spread his hands wide. "Following people, listening at keyholes, hunting for clues...."

"Oh, that." Emma said. "There is a 90 per cent probability that such a task will be part of our visit to the Lord Castlereagh's ball."

"Well, that's a relief, then." Killian drew a deep breath. He wasn't going to be another Lord Parkington, who disdained cryptography. He was going to understand this stuff if it killed him. It probably would kill him, but at least he would die knowing more than Parkington. "Why don't you start again from the beginning, and take it slowly?"

Her dazzling smile was reward enough.

After a while, some of the principles did sink in. Killian actually understood most of what Emma had explained. Some of it, anyway. But even if he never became as skilled as Emma, he had gained a new respect for her ability. She was as expert in cryptography as he was in swordplay. It would be a dull world if all people were the same.

Emma had begun packing up her papers to be returned to the safe, where he had been told they were kept, when Sophie brought in the post. "For you, Mademoiselle."

She handed the stack of letters to Emma, curtseyed and retreated.

Killian watched Emma sort through the letters. Most were for her aunt, Madame Scatha—handsome invitation cards and lengthy letters full of gossip. A handful of brief and businesslike missives were for her father, Lord Forgall. The final letter was addressed to her.

"Who is it from, then?" He looked over her shoulder.

The letter, written on plain, unremarkable stationery, was addressed simply to "Miss Forgall," with no other direction. A blob of wax held it closed. She slipped her pen knife under the wax and opened it. Spreading the single page flat, she studied the carefully penned message inside. Written in French, the message read,

"For information about Le Regent which has gone missing, come to the Café of the Four Cats tonight after nightfall. Ask to be conducted to the private parlor."

If ever Killian had seen a trap, this was one. It was an invitation to be murdered, pure and simple, and though he was quite willing to concede that Emma was talented with numbers and codes, he was certain she had no experience in dealing with a situation like this one.

He took the letter from her. "I shall go."

"No," she replied, "this was addressed to me. I shall go. Nobody asked you."

"You can't go out alone in Paris. Especially not to this café – I know where it is, and it's in a bad neighborhood. You're a woman, a young woman, and obviously rich and a foreigner – you wouldn't last five minutes."

"I'll wear a disguise," Emma said simply.

"I'll be thinking there is no disguise that will hide your soft white hands—"

"Gloves."

"And your plump soft cheeks and bright eyes—"

"Rouge and face paint."

"And your finishing-school French. Look, you are who you are, and no matter how you try, you can't cover it up. You're not starving, you're not dirty—"

Emma slapped the table with her open palm. "Why do you all insist on coddling me? Am I always to be wrapped in cotton-wool, prevented from doing anything worthwhile? Am I never to have a chance to decide anything for myself, to take a risk— to really live?"

He stared at her, open-mouthed. This crazed notion had truly lodged in her head. But he had heard this cry for independence from others, usually young men. He knew how desperate some people could be to prove themselves, and how dangerous it was to let them take the bit between their teeth and gallop straight into disaster.

"Fine. But you're not doing this alone, *mavourneen*. You need my help. We will make a plan. First we need a story about why you should be at this Inn of the Four Cats. Then, when we're there, I will let you do the talking, while I stand behind you and look menacing."

"Oh, you'll let me?"

"Be sensible," he begged. "You have never done anything like this before, have you?"

"Well—no." She frowned, looking mutinous.

"And I have, God forgive me for the young fool that I was. You know you need my help, so why not accept it?"

"Because you think you can take over and make all the decisions for my own good," she said bitterly. " But it's not for my own good. You don't know what my own good is. I demand that you respect my right to make my own choices."

This was bound to end in disaster, but Killian couldn't see any other alternatives. He comforted himself with the thought that he could bring in Leary as a backup, when trouble arose. "Very well, I'll respect you. I'll let – that is, I accept that you are in charge of this operation. Just let me go with you."

Relieved, she smiled at him, stretching out one hand to give his forearm a squeeze of thanks. "Very good. This is wonderful. Thank you so much."

"Anything for you, *mavourneen*." He must be out of his mind. At least he had Leary to fall back on.

"But you must promise me one thing."

"Yes?"

"You must promise not to tell Lieutenant Leary."

His jaw dropped open. "What?"

"Promise me! Please." She clasped her hands together in supplication. "You know that Leary will tell Fiona, and she's certainly not up to the challenge."

Killian shook his head. "Leary must be involved. Someone has to drive us there, and I'm certainly not going to that place on foot."

"But we must keep Fiona from finding out," she insisted.

"Sure and that's a promise. At least one member of this crack-brained crowd must be kept from running headlong into danger."

11

Emma looked around as Killian helped her creep quietly off the back of the borrowed hay wagon into the stable yard of the Inn of the Four Cats. Leary, dressed as a down-on-his-luck wagon driver in ragged clothes, reined in his team and acted oblivious to their presence. The yard was empty except for scattered piles of hay, but sounds of raucous activity spilled out of the small mullioned windows of the inn.

Emma brushed as much of the hay off her dark cloak as she could. Gloves made her hands clumsy when it came to picking off stray bits that had caught within the weave of the fabric, and she gave an annoyed tsk. Killian's grip on her elbow tightened. His expression was alert and his gaze traveled quickly around the empty space.

"What are you looking for?"

"Nothing." He steered her quickly toward the inn's entrance. She knew he wasn't telling her the truth, but there wasn't time to object. And besides, insisting that he explain himself would only delay the meeting—which was the reason for being here in the first place.

The tavern bar was smoky and dark with a low ceiling. The occupants proved to be a motley collection of foreign soldiers, tattered Parisian bottom-feeders, and a few wide-eyed farmers in from the French countryside. Emma fancied she saw suspicion shining in their eyes. She told herself it was just a trick of the firelight, but pulled the tattered hood of her cloak farther over her face.

There was no need to worry. Nobody could recognize her.

She was in disguise. The dark cloak purchased earlier from a rag-picker's stall covered her from head to hem, while under it she wore the kitchen maid's oldest floor-scrubbing dress. Killian, in a country gentleman's tweed suit, looked much more conspicuous than she did. He hadn't even bothered to dirty up his face. After complaining that she looked too clean!

It was too late now to change his well-groomed and prosperous appearance, or to change her mind on his presence by her side. The note had instructed Emma to come alone, but Killian had stubbornly insisted on coming with her. After a lengthy argument she'd given in. She hoped that his presence would not discourage their contact from revealing the information that she wanted to know.

The innkeeper bustled up to them.

"Your best private room," Killian ordered arrogantly.

Emma ground her teeth. They had agreed that she would do the talking.

The innkeeper bowed. "Yes, of course, milord. We've just the room available and a chicken fricassee for dinner." The fellow raised one thick black eyebrow and stroked a finger along his mustache. "Also, just between us, milord, I have a certain quantity of excellent Irish whiskey. For discerning patrons, you understand."

Emma frowned. How did the fellow know that Killian wanted Irish whiskey?

"Just what we need," Killian replied.

"Right this way, milord."

Before mounting the stairs to the private room, Emma scanned the crowd. One man of especially evil aspect was leering directly at her. She quickly looked away and followed Killian.

Upstairs, the innkeeper flung a door open with a flourish and gestured for them to enter. The room was small and dingy, with a window that overlooked the inn yard and a fireplace with sooty black streaks that climbed up to the mantel. The table and chairs, set on a braided rag rug, looked worn but sturdy. Shoved against the wall in the far corner of the room, covered with an old quilt, was a bed.

Did the innkeeper think they were lovers? He was mistaken. This was a business meeting, pure and simple.

Emma began, "But—"

"Never mind," interrupted Killian.

"It is our best chamber," the innkeeper said, looking a bit hurt.

Emma clamped her mouth shut. Arguing would simply make it easier for the innkeeper to remember her, and the one thing she wanted was to be invisible. She was a spy, but she had never been out in the field before. Her cryptography skills were a form of spying, but it was work that had to be conducted in a safe, private environment. She knew what other spies had told her—but how did she know they were telling her the truth? She wanted to feel certain that the information she was passing along was accurate, and not twisted by the intelligence-gatherer's perceptions. This was worth the risk. She was capable. She could do it.

The innkeeper bowed himself out.

"I don't think you needed to come along at all," she told Killian as she sat down at the table and put back her hood. "I could have ordered a private room all by myself."

"If you had, the innkeeper would have taken you for a lady of the night," Killian informed her. "No other woman would bespeak a private room at this tavern."

"But he thinks that anyway," Emma pointed out reasonably. "He thinks you and I are having an affair!"

"That can't be helped," Killian replied. "But you're supposed to be invisible. You shouldn't have spoken at all. We don't want him to be able to identify you."

She crossed her arms. "I am still not convinced. The message said—"

A knock on the door made Emma put up her hood again. She turned to look out the window. Killian was probably right about not letting the innkeeper see her. In the inn yard, the wagon full of hay had drawn up under their window and the ragged driver was arguing with one of the hostlers.

How frustrating to finally be out in the field, but unable to do anything. This was nearly as bad as being stuck at home— even though she definitely wasn't at home, and her father would be furious if he knew. She was his most efficient secretary, his code breaker, his princess, his pawn. Moreover, he would be horrified to know that she was alone in a tavern room with a man. But it wasn't like that. Killian was a very attractive man, but she was here to gather information, not to indulge in a midnight tryst with a handsome Irishman.

Dinner was delivered, along with the promised whiskey. Her stomach rumbled. The chicken smelled delicious, but it seemed so wrong to sit down to a meal when they should be on the alert for their visitor.

Killian smiled at her. "Have a seat, *mavourneen.*"

"No. Someone has to watch for our contact."

Her haughty response should have stung him, should have reminded him of his intelligence-gathering responsibility. Instead, he sat down and spread his napkin over his lap. "Suit yourself."

For the next few minutes, she stared down into the stable yard. She heard the clinking of pewterware on pottery, followed by a long hum of satisfaction. Emma pressed her lips together. The hay-wagon was still in the same place under their window. Now a shawl-covered female had hurried into the yard, seen the wagon, and begun to berate the driver for some misdeed.

"Here, try this." Killian startled her by appearing at her side, offering her a spoonful of food. The aroma of the chicken was too enticing to resist. Taking the spoon from him, she tasted the dinner and found it good. "The fellow you're waiting on won't arrive for a while, so you might as well eat."

She was hungry, after all. Following him back to the table, she asked, "How do you know the letter came from a he? And how do you know he won't arrive in the next few minutes."

He spooned chicken stew onto her plate and returned to his own meal. Between bites he said, "One, the innkeeper. Not sure where he came from, but since he's not a Frenchman, so he could very well be an agent for some government or other. Two, there are a fair number of soldiers from a variety of Allied armies downstairs, which again leads me to suppose that this is not a watering-hole for locals. And three, most of the foreigners in France are male, so whoever wrote you that note is very likely male also. More wine?"

She covered her wine glass with her hand. She'd had much more than she was used to drinking already. "No thank you. But how do you know he won't come right away?"

He set the carafe down. "There are a number of possibilities. He might have some other engagement to attend to before meeting you. Maybe he doesn't want to arrive too soon after you did. Or maybe he's a friend of the innkeeper and the innkeeper wants to earn his money for the meal."

"Or maybe you were just feeling peckish, so you are making up all these excuses," Emma countered with a smile. A warm glow spread through her and she was feeling less nervous. Being a spy in the field wasn't so bad. The informant would come, they would talk to him, and she would pay him the money she'd brought. If she moved just right, she could feel the gold coins hidden in the secret pocket under her dress. This spying business was rather exciting.

Captain Killian leaned back in his chair and watched her, running one finger over his full, well-shaped lips. "You know you could have left this up to me."

The standing candelabras in the corners of the room spread a warm, intimate glow. The noise of the tavern patrons downstairs was muted to a throbbing murmur. The very air around them seemed to beat with the very pulse with life.

"Why should I?" She lifted her chin. His intent gaze made her senses tingle. But that was wrong of her. He was no polite, well-behaved gentleman who respected the conventions of society. He had single handedly fought those soldiers on the bridge. He had plunged recklessly into a duel at the opera, for Heaven's sake. What would it be like to be kissed by this wild man, this man without fear, a man who indulged his passions?

But could she trust him, the doubting part of her brain asked. He might have chosen to do what Lord Parkington had asked of him—maybe he agreed with that view of himself as a soldier who was trained to kill without conscience. Then again, she had it on good authority that anyone who followed Lord Parkington's lead was a fool, and Killian certainly didn't appear to be a fool. She put the probability of his being in league with Parkington at about ten percent.

She considered him. He had an exuberant nature, dark good looks, and an excellent record as a military officer. He also had a loyal friend, and the fact that Lieutenant Leary liked and trusted him said a lot for his good character. So the likelihood that kissing him would turn out well...she put that at about eighty percent. No, that was the wine. No more than seventy-five percent. Seventy, if she were to be prudent.

Killian leaned over to her, distracting her from her calculations. He took her hand, gloved in her darkest kid-leather gloves. "Why should you have left this up to me? Because you are a beauty and a temptation, and as innocent as a babe in arms."

She tried to tug her hand free, but he held her fingers tight. With his other hand, he began to peel back the glove to expose the soft underside of her wrist. He stroked his fingers delicately across her flesh, causing her to shiver. "I agreed to your being here, because I intended to accompany you, to protect you. But now I've discovered a fault in my plan. Who will protect you from myself?"

"Stop it!" Instantly, he let her go. Her heart was beating in her ears, as if she'd almost stepped off a cliff. She snapped, "Have you no honor at all?"

"Oh, I have some honor left, and that's the very pity of it," Captain Killian said shaking his head regretfully. "But here you are, sweet and fresh as an April morning and thinking it's all a lark. 'Tis the big bad world you've stumbled into, *asthore,* and there's worse men than me."

She tossed her head. "If you tried anything, my father would hear of it."

"Have you told your father what you've been up to?" Killian said pointedly. "Does he know you're here?"

This truth made her squirm, but before she could think up a retort, there was a knock at the door.

Killian rose to his feet. Emma stood up as well, smoothing the front of the worn old gown with her palms. She needed to catch her breath. The door opened, admitting the innkeeper and a serving maid who cleared away the dinner plates.

As they left, a figure slipped in through the door. Underneath the black shawl that covered her head was the small, weaselly looking lady-in-waiting who'd accompanied Baroness Olga to the opera. The woman's sharp, narrow features and graying hair had faded into insignificance beside her glamorous mistress. Emma leveled a triumphant look at Killian—he certainly had been wrong about their anonymous correspondent being a man.

"*Mein Herr, meine Dame,*" Baroness Olga's companion said with a quick and nervous curtsey. So she was German, and not Russian like the woman who employed her.

Emma could not contain her surprise. "You are the one who sent the message? Do you have the diamond?"

"*Nein*," the woman said. "I did not say that I had it. Only that I knew where it is. That is enough. My information is valuable to you, *nicht wahr*?"

Killian demanded, "Were you followed here?"

"No. I do not think so," The woman said. "I am not sure. I do not have much time. Give me one hundred francs and I will tell you how to get the diamond."

Emma exclaimed, "One hundred francs?"

"Hush." Killian directed his attention to the woman. "One hundred francs for a hint about where to look for the Regent diamond? You work for Baroness Olga. I could make a wild guess and pay nothing."

The woman shrugged. "You can do what you like, but it will cost you time and effort. I can tell you the best way, the quickest way to get it back."

Killian crossed his arms over his chest. "Very well. I will offer you ten francs."

"Bah. That is nothing." The woman turned on her heel.

"Wait!" Emma said, extracting coins from her hidden pocket. "I can offer you twenty francs." She held them out.

The woman grabbed the money and it vanished into her dark, old-fashioned skirts. "Very well. Lord Castlereagh's ball."

"What about it?" Emma asked.

"The gem will change hands at the ball. Ugh, you British." The woman shook her head in annoyance, and spoke as if she were addressing a child. "It is not possible to search my lady's house for the gem. That is foolish. If you want it, you'll have to intercept it. At the ball. When it changes hands."

Killian said astonished. "You think she will be wearing the Regent diamond at Lord Castlereagh's ball?"

"I do not know that, just that it will be given to –" the woman threw a look over her shoulder. "What's that?"

A clatter of boots and the steely slither of swords being drawn sounded in the hallway. Killian grabbed Emma's arm and hauled her out of her chair.

Time to go," he said.

Killian had been right. Luckily, the ambushers wore heavy boots designed by General Blücher; sturdy footwear, but which made it hard for the wearer to sneak up on anyone.

"*Mein Gott!*" Baroness Olga's companion jumped at the heavy treads outside the door. "They are coming!"

Still holding on to Emma, Killian stepped over to the small window over the stable yard and threw open the sash.

"She's getting away," Emma shrieked, and broke free from his grasp.

Killian turned to see their informant pounding on the wood paneling of the room. With a click, a panel opened in the wainscoting. Just as Emma reached her, the woman slipped through the opening. The panel closed on Emma, trapping part of her skirt. With a growl, she pulled at the fabric to free herself, but the sturdy old work dress remained stuck.

Two burly thugs burst through the door.

"It's time to say goodbye," the first fellow said with an evil grin.

The men's swords were not gentlemen's rapiers like the one Killian wore. These were heavy broadswords that gleamed in the wavering candlelight. Emma cursed and yanked harder on her skirt.

Killian drew his sword and lunged at the first thug. The fellow parried and fought back, showing unexpected skill. Sending up a quick prayer that Emma would be safe for a few moments longer, Killian focused on matching the fellow's ferocious attack.

Killian's heart was in his mouth as he forced himself to focus on the opponent in front of him. This was why delicate females should stay safely at home. While he was fighting this one, what was the other thug doing? He didn't dare look.

A loud rip, followed by a scream and a scuffle, ended with a deep, hollow bong. Desperately, Killian took a chance and slipped his blade past his opponent's guard. The point sank deep into his shoulder. The fellow howled and clutched his injury. Killian pulled his sword free and whipped around to come to the rescue.

Emma, her hem hanging in rags, stood over her fallen attacker with a brass chamber pot in her hands. Stooping, she banged the heavy pot against the thug's head a second time, then dropped it and picked up his broadsword. She waved the weapon at another thug who had appeared in the doorway, shouting, "Don't come any closer!"

The thug in the doorway grinned. "Hello, pretty lady."

"How dare you?" Emma swung the sword at him. It pulled her off balance, but she recovered quickly.

A shout sounded from outside the window, the signal that Killian had been waiting for.

"Come on," Killian growled, dragging Emma away from her prey. "Out the window."

Another pair of attackers pushed into the room, causing the one in front to stumble over the fallen body of Emma's assailant.

"What?" Emma shrieked. "Are you crazed?"

Killian took the sword from her hand and threw it down. "You don't need that. No time to argue. Now off you go." He grabbed her around the waist and pushed her through the open window as more thugs piled into the room.

She held onto the sash, resisting his efforts to get her out. "What are you doing?"

"Jump!"

To his relief, she jumped. He swung his legs over the sill and followed her just as the thugs reached the window.

He landed in the back of the hay wagon, right beside her. The driver snapped his whip and the wagon lurched forward as the horses sprang into motion. A heavy body landed on the cobbles behind the wagon and the other thugs howled in fury from the window as the horses sped out of the stable yard and into the Paris night.

Emma groaned and lifted her head to glare at him. An errant stalk of hay fell over her eye and she blew it away. "You are a madman."

Killian tilted his head to one side and considered her words as the wagon jolted over rocks and swayed to a stop in a darkened alley. "You're not the first to suggest as much."

The winded horses' heads hung low, chests heaving as they blew air out through their nostrils. The driver of the wagon turned to address them. "Well, then, that was exciting."

"Well done, Leary," Killian said. "How did you manage to keep the information from dear Miss Fiona?"

"Keep it from me?" Fiona said. The woman beside Leary on the wagon bench turned, lowering the black scarf that had concealed her features. "You don't think that any of you could keep something like this from me?"

Emma pushed herself to her knees and glared at Killian. "You said Leary wasn't going to tell Fiona about the meeting!"

"I told him not to tell Fiona," Killian defended.

"I shouldn't have let you come with me in the first place!"

"'I didn't tell Miss Fiona," Leary added, looking hurt. "She followed me, 'struth she did."

Fiona's normally sweet face was transformed by her ferocious scowl. "How could you leave me out, Emma? I was the one who recognized the Regent Diamond for what it was. And if the informant had brought you the jewel, how would you have known if it was real, or only paste?" She brandished a small bronze instrument. "Did you remember to bring a jeweler's loupe with you? I thought not."

"You see what I was up against," Leary said to Killian.

"Aye," Killian replied.

Fiona continued, "It is clear to me that we cannot continue in this secretive way. We all wish to defend our nation, and the peace of the world. We must find a way to work together, and not conceal important information from one another. Are we agreed?"

Killian shook his head. "It would be much better if you just told us whatever you learned, and leave the rest to us. You may be experienced at code-breaking and the like," he nodded toward Emma, "but Leary and I are experienced fighters."

"No," declared Emma. "I won't let you go off without me, and sit at home not knowing what has happened. What if you miss clues or make mistakes because I wasn't there? We must work together."

Killian and Leary exchanged glances. Reluctantly, Killian said, "Very well. We will try it your way. For now."

Upon returning to Madame Scatha's residence, the four of them gathered in the front salon.

"Where are the horses and the wagon?" Fiona asked Leary.

"Back where I found them," he replied with a smile.

"They'll be all right for now."

"Now, for our next step, we should—" Killian began.

"The Castlereagh ball is too soon," Emma said, pounding her fist on the table in frustration. "Our chances of intercepting the Regent Diamond when it changes hands are too small. We would do better to search Baroness Olga's house."

"Our informant assured us that we'd never find her hiding place," Killian reminded her, "and that Baroness Olga was definitely bringing the diamond to Lord Castlereagh's ball."

"I knew that woman had it," Fiona said.

Emma nodded. "We were always going to attend Lord Castlereagh's ball. We'll get the diamond back once we're there."

"How?" Killian demanded.

"We will think of something," Emma said airily.

12

Emma stood up from the desk and stretched. She was still a little sore from her adventure of the night before. That wagonload of hay had proved not to be quite as soft as she might have wished. Not only that, but she had chosen last evening's adventure in spying over a growing pile of communiqués that needed deciphering. This morning had been dedicated to catching up on her work.

The difficulty was that now the communiqués had to be placed on her father's desk when he wasn't looking. He was already upset by her having left the earlier stack in the study, and she didn't want to disappoint him again. But it would have to be carefully managed. The work should have been finished and waiting for him when he walked into the safe room this morning, and now they were late. With any luck, she would be able to slip them onto his desk before he returned from his meeting with the Duke of Wellington. She quietly made her way down the stairs to the first floor to the safe room in which her father worked.

Muted voices were coming from inside the safe room. Emma's heart dropped. Heavens! He was already there. She stopped outside the door to gather her courage. She had about a sixty percent chance that he would fail to notice what she was doing, provided she behaved as if everything was completely normal.

The walls and door were thick enough to mute all but the human rumble of sound. She couldn't tell what was being said, just that one voice had the timbre of her father's speech, and the other... she wasn't sure. Drawing a calming breath, she arranged a confident smile on her face and then knocked on the door before pushing it open.

"Good morning, Papa," she said cheerfully. A quick glance identified the other occupant of the room as Lord Parkington. She nodded politely in his direction. " Good morning, sir."

She crossed the room, with its leather club chairs and ceiling-high ranks of bookshelves and file cabinets, and laid the communiqués on the usual corner of the desk. The room was bare of ornamentation, with one large map on the wall. It was also fairly dusty, since Lord Forgall did not allow the maidservants to clean it. He only permitted Emma or Fiona to sweep and dust under his own personal supervision, and then only after repeated pleas to be allowed to "do something" about the room.

The conversation had been interrupted when she entered, but once they had reassured themselves that it was only Emma, they relaxed. After a moment Lord Parkington said, "I know you have your reservations, sir, but hear me out. Let the Continentals handle their own troubles! Britain has her own interests at home to attend to. Tsar Alexander is a progressive leader and even Lord Castlereagh calls him a man of grand qualities—"

"Nonsense," Lord Forgall said. "The Tsar is already the most powerful ruler in Europe. Why should he be given more countries to rule over? There's no need to encourage his imperial ambitions. We just got rid of one Emperor."

"His reign over any additional territories, like Poland, would be as a form of benevolent despotism to begin with," Lord Parkington argued. "Because they need a strong leader. Many of these countries are not ready for a free society like we have in England. But that would change over time. The Tsar is a liberal, one might even say a revolutionary, at heart. He can bring them along gradually."

"Liberal, you say? Bah. Right now, the Tsar cherishes a fond belief in the universal rights of man," Lord Forgall said. "But once he discovers the vexations of governing a free society, he'll change his tune."

Emma had already heard this argument many times before. Tsar Alexander had changed his political tune several times already. First he opposed Napoleon, then he allied with him, and then opposed him again. Furthermore, some of the communiqués she had deciphered spoke of his increasing interest in mysticism and religiosity, fueled by his friendship with the Baroness von Krudener and Henri-Louis Empaytaz. She placed the folder of finished communiqués in their proper spot and glided toward the door.

"You can't be sure of—"

Lord Forgall waved a dismissive hand. "Besides, why would Britain allow it? You know the Tsar will not stop with Poland and the smaller Baltic countries. Russia needs more access to more warm-water ports from which to launch their navy and trading vessels. We'd have a new Empire right on our doorstep."

"They won't do that," Lord Parkington countered. "If you would just speak to Lord Castlereagh—"

Lord Forgall shook his head. "I will not. And you will hold your tongue on this matter as well, Parkington. You are dismissed."

"Yes, my lord." Lord Parkington gave a curt bow and followed Emma out of the room.

This would be a good opportunity to see if she could discover what Lord Parkington's real purpose was. So far, she had heard him insinuate that he wished to commit violence toward Monsieur Talleyrand, and now he was arguing on behalf of Russian expansion into Europe. She didn't dare tell her father her suspicions—not yet, when Lord Forgall still viewed this man as his successor. Her father would simply confront Parkington, and there was a good seventy to seventy-five percent chance he would believe Parkington and not herself. She would have to move cautiously.

She smiled at Parkington as they walked down the hall. "I know you. You are not going to give up your views, you're going to find a way to prove you're right. What exactly do you have up your sleeve?"

"I would never disobey Lord Forgall's exact orders," Lord Parkington said huffily.

"No, never," she agreed. "But you do mean to continue to advocate for what you feel is right?"

"Certainly. Just because the old—" he stopped himself. She kept an innocent smile pinned to her lips, and tried to look sympathetic. He sighed. "Well, there are ways of convincing

Lord Castlereagh that do not depend on my talking to him."

"Such as?"

Impulsively, Lord Parkington pulled her into the charming little parlor Madame referred to as her sewing-room. Baskets of stockings to be darned were lined up against the wall, and shelves held bolts of fabric and notions. He carefully shut the door.

"You're not to breathe a word of this, but Castlereagh and the Tsar have a great deal in common, if they could only see it," Lord Parkington whispered.

Emma's jaw dropped. She frowned and shook her head.

"Follow me closely here. The Tsar has been scouring the Bible for omens and signs that he is destined to rule all of Europe, whether outright or through some sort of a holy alliance based on religious principles. And Lord Castlereagh himself sincerely believes in the supernatural. I don't know if you remember his story about his encounter with the Radiant Boy, when he was staying overnight at the house of a friend in Ireland."

"Radiant Boy?" Emma asked. "What on Earth?"

"It's an omen," he explained. "A portent of doom called the Radiant Boy, a glowing, fiery figure of young man. It is said that the person who sees the Radiant Boy is doomed to death and destruction if he follows his present course of action."

"That's a folk tale," Emma objected.

"But Lord Castlereagh believes in it. He says he's seen one. And if he were to be visited by the Radiant Boy again, he might be persuaded to change course and support Tsar Alexander's approach to settling the Polish-Saxon Crisis."

"You're never going to try a trick like that," Emma said, aghast. "Britain won't allow the Tsar to gobble up Poland! We signed a treaty!"

"Shh. Treaties can be changed," Lord Parkington said soothingly. He stroked Emma's cheek with the back of his hand. "My plan will work. The reward will be substantial. And then, my dear Emma, I shall make you my wife."

Emma sighed. Lord Parkington had never believed her when she'd told him she didn't feel that way about him. He'd never paid attention to her gentle hints or even her kindly-worded refusals. He simply had to be made to see the truth.

Gently she removed his hand. To focus his attention

completely upon her, she placed her hands on either side of his face and gazed into his eyes. "Lord Parkington, hear me now. I can never, I will never be your wife. My heart is pledged to- to Captain Stephen Killian."

"You are to stay in the ballroom or the refreshment room at all times," Lord Forgall instructed his daughters as the carriage jolted through the Parisian streets toward Lord Castlereagh's residence for the ball. "I don't know why Madame Scatha couldn't watch over you at this event. But there you have it, and I've got an important meeting to attend so I trust you will act with the decorum I expect."

"Yes Papa," Fiona said obediently.

Emma drew in a breath. "Papa, I have to tell you that Lord Parkington—"

Lord Forgall waved his hand. "Never mind, my dear. I leave your choice of dancing-partners up to you, but remember that virtuous women do not waltz."

"Oh, Papa! Everybody waltzes these days," Fiona said with a little pout. Emma smiled at her sister. Fiona's preference for the big red-headed driver, Lieutenant Leary, was becoming more marked with every passing day.

"And if everyone were to jump off a cliff, would you do that too? Men embracing women in public, holding them in their arms as they whirl around—that's not dancing. It's a scandal." Lord Forgall harrumphed.

Emma stifled a laugh. "We'll be careful, Papa." She winked at Fiona. As a matter of fact, their father would spend no time whatsoever in the ballroom, and wouldn't bother with any gossip about whether his daughters had waltzed or not. "But I ought to tell you—"

"Later, my dear. Whatever it is, it can wait until after the meeting, if you please."

There was probably no need for Emma to worry about what Lord Parkington had told her. Surely it could wait until the morning. In the meantime, Emma had other matters to attend to at the ball.

The first of these was, *what would she say to Captain Killian?* The heat of a blush crept up her cheeks as she thought about how she'd told Lord Parkington that she was pledged to the Captain. It wasn't true—Captain Killian had paid her some flattering attentions, but he certainly hadn't asked for her hand in marriage. But Lord Parkington was the kind of man who wouldn't take "no" for an answer, and the Captain's name had simply popped out of her mouth.

It was an odd feeling, though, to admit to herself that she did have feelings for Captain Killian. She wouldn't ever admit as much to him—oh, no! That would be unthinkable. But uncomfortable as it was to face the fact that she'd told a fib, she felt comforted by the fact that Lord Parkington and Captain Killian hardly ever spoke to one another. That put the probability of Parkington ever telling the Captain what she'd said was less than five percent.

The carriage swept through the *porte cochère*, and they had arrived at the ball.

Lord Castlereagh's luxurious *"hotel particulier"* stood with its doors flung open to admit his high-ranking guests, who descended from gilt carriages and streamed into its elegant interior. Ladies in the latest fashions of high-waisted gowns and wearing ostrich feathers in their hair entered on the arms of dandies in satin knee-breeches and gold embroidered trim. Everywhere, men in military jackets and highly-polished boots strutted and twirled their mustaches.

"Emma, wait," Fiona said, catching her sister's arm. "Your lace sleeve is crooked. Let me fix it."

Emma stood still as Fiona fussed, rearranging the ivory lace on the tiny cap sleeve of Emma's dress. Snowy white didn't suit her complexion, so instead she had chosen a dress of apricot-colored silk with embroidery in old gold and touches of lace at her sleeves and low neckline. A string of pearls hung around her neck and a few jeweled pins flashed in her dark hair. "Done?"

"There. You look gorgeous," Fiona said, patting her shoulder lightly.

"You look gorgeous-er," Emma said, making Fiona giggle. But it was true. Fiona looked lovely in a pale blue gown that gave her an ethereal, fairylike glow.

The young Princess Dorothea of Courland, companion to Monsieur Talleyrand and married to his nephew, swooped over to them. "Oh, Miss Forgall, Miss Fiona, how marvelous this all is, don't you think? It's almost like Vienna!"

Her bubbling energy and bright brown eyes lifted Emma's spirits. Dorothea was a petite and energetic woman with a gamine spirit. Though her husband, Edmond de Perigord-Talleyrand, ignored her, she was very close to his uncle, the Foreign Minister. The distinguished diplomat was known for his lavish dinner parties and other entertainments, and in his company, Princess Dorothea de Courland had quickly developed into a superb hostess.

"Did you enjoy your time in Vienna?" Emma asked.

"Oh, yes!" Dorothea said brightly. "So many parties, such handsome men! You definitely should go."

Beside Emma, Fiona bounced up and down, waving vigorously at the opposite end of the ballroom. "Oh, look! It's Lieutenant Leary. Hello!"

"*Mon Dieu!* What an enthusiast your sister is," Dorothea said with a laugh. She stood on tiptoes. "Who is she waving to? I can't see."

"The tall one with the ginger hair," Emma said. Lieutenant Leary was plowing through the crowd, his flaming red hair easily visible above everyone else's.

"If it were up to me, I would pick the other, that one with the dark hair who accompanies him," Dorothea commented. "That strong chin, those lovely wide shoulders! Brr!"

Emma looked closer, and sure enough, there was Captain Killian following in the path that Leary had cleared. Her heart gave a little leap of excitement, but not wanting to arouse Dorothea's keen instincts, she gave a non-committal hum.

Too late. Dorothea glanced at her and smiled knowingly. "Aha! I knew such a one as he would not have escaped your notice. Who is he?"

"Captain Killian, late of the Inniskilling Dragoons, if I recall correctly," Emma muttered.

By that time, Lieutenant Leary had reached them. He stopped in front of Fiona, looking down at her with a silly grin on his face.

Fiona blushed. "Hello."

"Aye," Leary said, nodding. "Hello."

"Miss Forgall, 'tis a pleasure to see you again," Captain Killian said with a smile.

Before Emma could say anything, Dorothea stuck out her hand to Killian, leading with her wrist. "You beautiful man, I know my so-dear friend Emma would not wish to keep you all to herself. I am the Princess de Courland, but you may call me Dorothea."

Killian delicately grasped her fingers and bowed over them, brushing his lips over her gloved knuckles. "'Tis truly honored I am to be allowed to bask in your radiant beauty, Princess."

Dorothea giggled. "Oh, an Irishman! And with the gift of – of how do you say it? Gab, is it not? The gift of gab."

He laid one hand on his heart. "On the bones of Saint Brigid herself, I confess you've struck me dumb with your wit and splendor, my lady. Princess, I should be saying."

Emma rolled her eyes.

Dorothea snapped open her fan and fanned herself. "Well! Now I see why Emma hides you away. Well, you must come and visit me sometime, *non?*"

"Dorothea is the wife of Monsieur Talleyrand's nephew," Emma informed him.

"Now there's a wonderful thing," Killian said heartily. "I met Monsieur Talleyrand just the other day. Quite a remarkable fellow."

Emma eyed him suspiciously, not sure what to make of such bland praise. Did he admire Talleyrand or not?

Dorothea, however, was not at all ambiguous about her feelings for her husband's uncle. "Remarkable indeed. He is the most amazing of creatures. No one appreciates him fully, except those of us who are closest to him. He is so cool and controlled in all circumstances, and yet beneath that cool exterior is a blazing, brilliant mind and a bold temperament that enjoys danger in all its forms. It is that very contrast that makes him so appealing."

Emma could see that Killian was paying close attention to Dorothea's words. Could it be that Killian wanted to find that same balance within himself, a cool exterior with a passionate heart? That cool exterior was so necessary to a spy, who must control himself perfectly.

Dorothea went on. "They call him *le diable boiteux*, the lame devil, and they do not trust him because he has served both royalty and revolutionaries—but it is I who tell you, Captain, that he serves always France, no matter what the regime."

Killian bowed very deeply. "The Morrigan herself would not be a better champion for Monsieur Talleyrand than your fine self, Princess."

With a charming smile, Dorothea swept herself away, looking very pleased.

As Emma turned to resume her conversation with Captain Killian, Lord Parkington interrupted. "I'd like a word with you, if I may."

His tone was curt, and he completely ignored Captain Killian. He had been very angry with her for rejecting him earlier in the day. Emma felt sorry for hurting him, and wished she could explain that she'd been completely at a loss about how else to tell him that his interest wasn't returned, since he hadn't picked up on any of her gentle hints. Judging from his haughtiness, he had finally gotten the message, so perhaps she could return to a more gentle tone. Would it hurt less if he knew that she'd felt compelled to be blunt, as a last resort? Perhaps she ought to try. Emma began, "I do wish to apologize—"

Killian stepped in between them. "Anything you say to Miss Forgall you can say to me. She knows she can rely on me."

"Begone," Lord Parkington ordered, stiff-arming Killian. "Her father approves of me. You have no right to interfere in our private conversation."

"Now wait just a moment," Emma began indignantly. All thoughts of apologizing to him vanished from her mind.

Killian moved Lord Parkington's arm out of the way, pushing toward him until they were nose to nose. "Would you like to step outside?"

Lord Parkington backed off with a scornful look. "Fisticuffs. Is that all you barbarians can think of?" He turned to Emma and grasped her by the wrist. "Do not think you can brush me off so easily. Matters are moving faster than expected, and after tonight, I will have good cause to call you mine."

"Let go of me," Emma said through gritted teeth.

Lord Parkington released her. He bowed. "Until later, my dear."

Before she could say anything, he turned on his heel and walked away.

13

Killian's fists curled into tight bunches, but he unclenched them and took a few calming breaths. A spy did his work subtly and inconspicuously. A spy did not call attention to himself by beating that smarmy *spalpeen* Parkington to a pulp, satisfying though that would be. Parkington disappeared into the card room, probably gone to tell tales to Lord Forgall about what that Irishman was doing, playing up to his daughter.

Killian gave himself a mental shake. After that unpleasant scene, Emma ought to be distracted, to have her spirits lifted. He could do that. Grinning broadly at her, he said, "It's breaking hearts you are tonight, Miss Forgall. May the divil himself snatch me away if you're not the prettiest lady in all of Paris, and that's the honest truth."

Emma blinked and drew a breath. She smiled. "Dorothea was right. You do have the gift of gab."

"Not a bit of it! I'm a simple plain-spoken fellow." He held out his hand. "May I have the honor of this waltz?"

"Oh, dear. Perhaps I should not," Emma said, pouting prettily. "My father says that virtuous women do not waltz."

"No, no. With all due respect to your distinguished sire, 'tis only virtuous women who waltz." Killian took Emma's hand, and she didn't resist as he drew her onto the dance floor. He could feel his tension and bad feelings fade away as he gazed into her lovely, eager face. She looked stunning tonight, her eyes sparkling like emeralds and her dark hair caught up into an elaborate arrangement with curls cascading down over her shoulders.

"How can that be?" Emma asked.

He slipped one arm around her waist and took her other hand in his. "Because gracefulness is a virtue, and a woman must be graceful in order to dance properly."

"And she must be nimble, to avoid her partner's treading on her toes," Emma said with a wide grin.

Killian nodded. "Graceful indeed. I shall do my utmost not to tread on your toes, my dear Miss Forgall."

The music started and he swung her into the dance. Emma waltzed very gracefully, following his lead with the ease of a practiced dancer. Just the lightest pressure on her waist was enough to signal a change in direction. He felt as if they had fallen by instinct or intuition into a natural, unspoken rhythm. They flowed together around the room, swept away by the beauty of the music until it seemed they were the only couple in existence.

"But you should not call me that," she murmured.

"Call you what?"

"Your dear," she said, her gaze cast down. "You said I was your dear Miss Forgall."

He bent his head, trying to look into her eyes. "But you are dear to me. You are a dear delight, a pearl beyond price."

She lifted her head at that. Her chin jutted out. "You needn't flatter me."

"I'm not."

Her gaze fell again, and they waltzed together in silence for a moment. The dancers swirled around them, flowing and eddying in time to the music like the billows on an ocean.

"Have you seen Baroness Olga here tonight?" Emma asked.

"No," he said lightly. "Not interested in any other ladies tonight."

"Be serious. We know she's here, and she is planning to hand over the Regent Diamond to someone at this very ball. We must find her and keep an eye on her."

"We can ask Leary to watch for her. And Miss Fiona," Killian said, giving Emma a light push so that she twirled under his arm. When he caught her in his arms again, he added, "That Parkington is the one to watch, I'm thinking. Do you trust him?"

Emma shook her head. "He told me the wildest story

about a plot against Lord Castlereagh."

"Lord Castlereagh?" Killian frowned. "Not Monsieur Talleyrand?"

Emma shook her head. "No, he intended to drive Lord Castlereagh out of the diplomatic corps using some supernatural omen."

What was Parkington up to? First Talleyrand, and now Lord Castlereagh. It sounded as if he were trying to sabotage the entire peace process.

"But, Captain Killian," Emma said, looking worriedly up at him, "whatever it was, Lord Parkington said that it would happen here. Tonight."

Killian stopped dancing. "Tonight?" Emma nodded. They stood in the middle of the ballroom, staring at each other in consternation. Other dancing couples sent annoyed glares their way as they maneuvered around them.

Emma squeezed his hand. "We have to do something."

Before Killian could reply, a woman in a blue silk turban swept by in the arms of an Austrian colonel. Her familiar Russian-accented voice called, "Oh, Captain! Why do you not dance?"

It was Baroness Olga, her white teeth bared in a malicious grin. Diamonds sparkled around her neck and at her earlobes. But then his gaze lifted to her headdress, and his heart nearly stopped. Nestled in the silken folds of her turban, a large gem winked at him.

"The Regent Diamond," he whispered.

The music ended and dancers milled about. Some went in search of refreshment, or out to the terraces for fresh air. Others slipped into the gardens for privacy. A few ladies retreated to the walls of the ballroom, fanning themselves. Baroness Olga, having freed herself from her Austrian colonel, sashayed up to them and languidly presented Killian with the back of her hand to be kissed.

Emma stared wide-eyed at the jewel in Baroness Olga's turban. "How could you?"

Baroness Olga fluttered her long eyelashes. "Too obvious? Perhaps, darling. But people are too blind to see."

"Perhaps they're too busy admiring your—your person," Emma retorted.

Killian had to agree. Baroness Olga had done a masterful job of distracting an onlooker's gaze away from her headgear.

Her dress was composed of nearly transparent white gauze with strategically placed designs of sequins and small rhinestones. Underneath, she wore nothing to speak of.

"Perhaps," Baroness Olga replied with a smirk, as she toyed with a small fan that hung from a cord around her wrist.

"You know what you're doing is wrong." Emma declared.

Baroness Olga lifted her eyebrows. "You do not like the dress?"

"I am referring to," Emma nodded toward the turban and dropped her voice to a whisper. "The stone. Give it back. It doesn't belong to you."

"You cannot order me to do anything," Baroness Olga gave a flick of her fan. "Do not bother your pretty head."

Emma's eyes went dangerously flat and her small white fingers curled into claws. Alarmed, Killian stepped forward. "Will you give me this dance, Lady Olga?"

"I would adore, Captain Killian. It is becoming very boring in here."

Grimacing horribly at Emma to signal that she shouldn't object, Killian hurried the Russian onto the dance floor. Baroness Olga's hand was warm in his and her smile gleeful and inviting, making him suspect he'd leaped from the frying pan into the fire this time. The hackles on the back of his neck rose. The heat of battle was far more preferable to the heat of this social engagement—the ballroom held all the danger, yet offered none of the release. Tensions rose but remained bottled up. The gauzy fabric of her dress slid disconcertingly under his palm.

"You are an excellent dancer," Baroness Olga said, breaking into his train of thought.

"As are you," he replied. Deeming it time to get on with his spying duties, he flashed a brief glance up at her turban. "Audacious of you to wear the Regent Diamond so openly. Quite a clever joke."

She threw her head back and laughed. "Ah, I am so glad you appreciate! It is so boring when men do not have a sense of humor."

"So what do you plan to do with it?"

She shrugged. "I am undecided. None of them loves me for myself, they only love me for what I can give. The French, they make love to me so nicely, is almost worth it to give them their diamond back. But my own country...well, it is my country, you understand. I know the Tsar, he likes his omens and symbols. And now I can give the Regent, which is symbol of a king's right to rule France. He will be grateful, maybe."

Killian gave her the widest, most seductive smile he could muster. "You're a magnificent woman, *acushla*, and the fellow who doesn't love you for your fine and beautiful self wouldn't be worth the having."

She threw her head back and laughed again in that full-throated way, then slapped him lightly on the shoulder. "Oh, you flatter so sweetly, I could almost believe it. But already I know how much money you have, and it makes me sad. Perhaps when I get my reward for the diamond, I shall take you as a lover."

The hair on Killian's head rose a little bit. "You wouldn't be forgetting that the Regent Diamond is cursed, now would you? Those who possess it come to bad ends. Like Queen Marie Antoinette, poor *creathur*, and the King, and all those others."

"Yes that was very sad," Baroness Olga said with a sigh. "But I do not believe in omens or curses. I am Olga, and I will make it a good-luck bringer for me."

"All alone, Fräulein Forgall?"

Emma turned her head to look at the tall, imposing Prussian officer smiling down at her. It was Freiherr Walter von Hentzow, who hd been part of the disastrous scene in the opera box. Emma ought be angry at von Hentzow. Madame Scatha said that they'd all been banned from the theater for the season, and that she'd very nearly been made to give up the box permanently.

Tonight, von Hentzow was the perfect picture of a Prussian Junker. His waist length, tight fitting blue jacket was crisscrossed with gold braid, and a short fur-trimmed cape swung carelessly from one shoulder. He clicked his heels together as he bowed. "Allow me to keep you company."

"Oh, well. That's so kind of you, but I was looking –

looking for Lord Parkington," Emma said.

The Prussian clucked his tongue. "You will excuse my saying, but that fellow is not a fit companion for a lady."

"Why? What do you know?" she demanded urgently.

From the Prussian's expression, Emma gathered that he was taken aback by her abruptness. She added, "That is, how terribly distressing to hear you say so. I do hope my father isn't putting too much trust in him." She batted her eyelashes at him for good measure.

He relaxed and smiled. "Ah. He is just ... untrustworthy. Not suitable for a well-bred lady to know. Keep this in mind."

"Well, thank you," Emma said, turning to go.

"Wait," the Prussian said. Emma stopped. "Where are you going? Are you not wishing to dance? I have not had the pleasure of a dance with you yet."

"I have to ... have to..." Unable to come up with an excuse, Emma turned her hands up helplessly and offered him an apologetic smile. "Perhaps later?"

"You will come and find me." It sounded more like an order than a request.

"Yes, yes." Emma sped toward the hall, more to get away from the Prussian than anything else. Once she'd rounded the corner, she leaned against the wall and took a deep breath.

The quiet hallway restored her equanimity. Lord and Lady Castlereagh's residence was beautiful, and untouched by the violence that had marred parts of Paris during the waning days of Napoleon's reign. Emma had been here before. The ballroom and other reception rooms were on this main floor. On the floor above were the bedchambers and a few sitting-rooms, and below were the kitchens, offices and other utilitarian spaces.

Where would one be most likely to lay an ambush for Lord Castlereagh? Emma guessed it would be upstairs, possibly near a bedchamber, to take advantage of the nighttime shadows and a host's weariness. Making as little sound as possible, she mounted the stairs.

The sounds of the ball faded away and soon she was stepping carefully down the dimly lit hallway. She stopped at the first door and quietly turned the handle. The room was empty and dark, so she closed the door again. She moved along to the next door and then the next. All was quiet.

Finally, at the end of the hallway, she heard someone moving around.

Placing her hand on the wood of the door to steady it, she turned the handle and opened the door a crack. She held her breath as she peered in, and then let it out when she realized this room, too, was empty. Opening the door a little wider, she stepped in to the room. A tiny flicker of light came from behind another door, probably leading to the valet's chamber. The light outlined masculine décor, and the scent of bay rum identified the room as Lord Castlereagh's bedchamber.

Emma stood still, not daring to move, afraid to bump into some unnoticed piece of furniture. The noises from the adjoining room continued, soft and unidentifiable. The valet, probably? Her mind raced, throwing up excuses in case she was caught. *Headache, looking for somewhere to lie down... my lady said I could rest in her bedchamber... oh, this is not her bedchamber? My goodness, what a mistake!*

Suddenly a brighter light flickered into existence in the darkened room. A single tongue of flame appeared in a corner of the chamber, dancing in mid-air. It winked out, and then reappeared, and slowly grew. Emma frowned, looking for the source of the flame, some candle or lamp. But there was none.

A shiver of fear raced up her spine. Where did the flame come from? Was there a candle there, resting on something she couldn't see? If it was a candle, how had it been lighted when there was no one there to light it?

The flame slowly grew, spreading into a ball of fire and then into a shape, a human form with blazing arms and a fiery head. The writhing, twisting flames gave the figure a horrible sense of life, and for and she thought she saw a face appearing in the rounded frame of the head. Terror rooted Emma to the spot, stole her breath until she was unable to scream or call out.

Suddenly, the fiery figure vanished. The visitation was over. Emma went limp, like a marionette whose strings had been cut. She leaned against the wall for support as her brain reeled. The room was just a dark, empty bedchamber again.

A low voice said, "Damn."

The ordinary curse slapped her in the face, hit her like a dash of cold water. She let out a gasp, and then clapped her hand over her mouth. Had she been heard? She waited, but it seemed the person in the valet's room had not heard her. Feeling behind her for the door, she carefully fumbled it open and crept out. Her legs wobbled under her as she returned to the main floor. He had done it. She didn't know how, but he had managed to lay his trap. He had to be stopped.

Skirting the edge of the ballroom, she made it through the French doors and onto the terrace without being stopped by an acquaintance, for which she was very grateful. Fiona and Lieutenant Leary were leaning against the stone balustrade talking quietly when she found them.

"Emma! Where have you been?" Fiona demanded.

"I found it. I saw what he's doing." Emma took Fiona by the arm. "Come. We have to stop him."

"Whisht now, Miss Forgall, don't you go off like a rocket," Leary said gently. "Let's take a moment to breathe. Then we'll find the Captain, quick as you please, and set about doing the thing right."

Killian stepped out onto the terrace and came over to Emma. "There you are! Where did you get off to? Twas with the divil's own making of excuses – pardon me language – that I finally got free of that overheated Russian lady, and then you'd vanished."

Emma reached her hand out to him pleadingly. "Oh, Captain Killian, you must come with me right now!"

"Well, 'tis flattered I am, to be sure, but I've got to tell you about what Baroness Olga said."

"Never mind about her! Fiona, you and the Lieutenant go look for Monsieur Talleyrand and ask him to deal with Baroness Olga. We must do something about Lord Parkington."

After a brief discussion, Fiona and Leary sped off on their errand, and Emma led Killian back up the stairs. At the top of the staircase, Emma stopped Killian and whispered, "You go first. Pretend to be Lord Castlereagh."

"And what is supposed to happen then?"

"I don't have time to explain it, but it's a sort of trick to frighten his lordship."

Killian huffed out an impatient sigh "Very well. It's not that I'm complaining, but it would be much better to know what to expect."

Emma patted his shoulder, and he strode down the hall and entered the bedchamber. She slipped in behind him and crouched down, watching with interest as he played the role of a man alone in his own bedchamber. He yawned and stretched, loosened his cravat, and rattled his sword as if taking it off.

Emma watched the corner where the mysterious light had appeared. The bedchamber was still dark, lit only by a single candle. Killian kept moving around, going through the motions, until suddenly the floating light appeared. Killian's gasp was every bit as astonished as she could have wanted.

The flame grew as it had before, shaped itself into a human-like form. It was frightening and yet Emma felt a sense of wonder. It defied all logic. How could it be happening? I couldn't be a real ghostly apparition, and if it wasn't, how was the effect produced?

Without warning, Killian unsheathed his sword and leapt forward with a shout. He slashed the blade through the flaming apparition. Nothing happened. A crash sounded from the valet's chamber. Killian pivoted and ran to the valet's door, shouting, "Stop him! He's going out the other way!"

Emma jumped up and opened the bedchamber door, but the hallway was empty. The struggle was behind her. She turned to see Killian fighting with Lord Parkington. A shrewd blow by Killian sent Lord Parkington reeling. He fell through the adjoining door, and into the valet's chamber, upsetting the apparatus he had set up in there. He slumped to the ground, knocked out.

"That's not very diplomatic," Emma said.

Killian stepped over Parkington's fallen form into the small space. "What is all this?"

Emma and Killian inspected the collection of materials in the valet's chamber, which included a mirror, a pot of steaming water over a brazier, and a lantern. Emma stamped out the coals that had fallen out of the brazier and straightened the lantern. Killian picked up a candle and, walking back into the bedchamber, went over to the corner where the glowing image had appeared. The candle's light revealed a large glass mirror with no frame propped in the corner.

"It was all just smoke and mirrors, then," Killian said.

"Just a trick."

Emma, who was still looking through the items in the valet's chamber, commented, "He must have sought advice from some theatrical person."

Lord Castlereagh himself stepped into his bedchamber. "What is going on here?"

Together Killian and Emma explained the plot to the bewildered Lord Castlereagh. He shook his head in disbelief. "An Englishman. A member of our own diplomatic corps," he kept saying.

Emma glanced over to the valet's chamber, where Parkington had lain. He was gone.

"Captain Killian!" Emma cried, pointing.

Killian bowed to Lord Castlereagh. "Begging your pardon, my lord, but we have to find him."

"I'll set the footmen to searching for him right away," Lord Castlereagh said. "One way or another, we'll find him, the blackguard."

14

Killian raced down the stairs and stopped at the bottom step. Which way would Parkington go? He looked to the left and right, considering his options. Emma's light footsteps sounded behind him, and she stopped at his side. Her color was high.

"He'd go out through the garden," she said. "We've been here many times before, and he knows there's a gate at the very back. He could slip out there, and not have to go back through the front rooms of the house."

"Very well," Killian said, and took Emma's hand. "That's where we'll look."

They slipped out the tall French doors and down the steps into the dark garden. The night was clear and the stars winked overhead like diamonds scattered on black velvet. The air was fresh, having lost the heaviness of daytime heat. Killian breathed in deep, the scents of yew and lavender from the ornamental knot-garden perfuming the night. He stepped out onto the gravel pathway with Emma at his side.

"In the daytime, it's a lovely place. In this section, he plantings make such pretty designs, with the colors so carefully tended."

"What else is here?" Killian asked.

"Well, there's a croquet lawn over there," she gestured, but he felt rather than saw the movement. "And the maze is down and to our left. The grotto is to the right. And the fountains are in the middle."

"Bless me," Killian remarked, amazed at how much fussy

effort had been put into the place. "How big is it?"

"Oh, quite large," Emma assured him.

"We'd better get started then. What's the quickest way to the back gate you mentioned?"

Emma stopped. "It's difficult to say. It looks so different at night. But I think it's this way."

They walked along the gravel pathway, well-lit by the silvery moon above. The fountains were still playing, even though most guests were inside. They passed the croquet lawn, which was empty, and peered into the grotto, which turned out to be a shallow little construction. There was no sign of Parkington at the back gate, so they retraced their steps. When they came to the maze, Emma stopped. "Do you think we should go in? I know the trick of it, but if you think we should go to the back gate and wait—"

"No," Killian said. "Castlereagh's footmen will be guarding the back gate by now. He won't get away from them. And if he's decided to hide rather than to run, this is a good a hiding place as any. "

They started into the maze, its tall green walls enclosing them fully as they entered. Emma led the way confidently, past several twists and turns, counting to herself as they went. Killian stopped by a small marble bench. "Let's sit here and talk a moment. We can rest, and he can't get past us, can he?"

Emma seemed reluctant as she sat down beside him. Then she relaxed and sighed. "It's rather a nice night to be out. Isn't it?"

"Yes," Killian said. Although he'd said that Parkington might have hidden himself in the maze, he didn't think it likely. He'd probably headed toward the back gate, and so the two of them could safely leave his capture up to Lord Castlereagh's footmen. Right now, he wanted to spend a little time alone with Emma.

"It's too bad we can't enjoy it. We have to keep looking, we can't give up now." Emma was restless as a cat, poised as if she were going to jump to her feet at any moment.

He sighed internally. Too bad she wasn't in a sitting and talking mood. "Then do you want to separate, and each of us look for him on our own?"

"No, no, I want to stay with you," she said, clutching his arm in a gratifying way. "We'd never find one another again.

"What are you so afraid of?" he teased her. "I am here to guard you and protect you, amn't I ?"

"No, I mean, yes," she said with a laugh. "I'm not afraid, but I don't want to be out here alone. It's—"

A couple burst around the corner of the maze and ran past them giggling. Killian watched their retreat with envy. They looked like they were having fun.

"You wouldn't be alone," he pointed out. "There'd be plenty of couples hiding around you."

"Never mind that. Oh, this is hopeless." Emma moved away from him on the bench and looked at him seriously. "I know what you've been asked to do. It's wrong. I can't believe my father would order it, so I believe these orders are from Lord Parkington alone. Are you still intending to carry out Lord Parkington's orders?"

Killian looked at her in astonishment. "That miserable fellow? You should know that I would never do anything that Parkington told me to do. What do you think you heard?"

"I don't have to think. I heard him tell you that Monsieur Talleyrand was a source of irritation to our government needed to be done away with so that England could make its own decision about the fate of France."

"You may have heard him say so, but you didn't hear me agree to that, because I never did."

Emma clutched her hands together and bowed her head over them. " I didn't hear you agree, but I was afraid you had."

"Well, I did not agree," he said hotly. "What sort of a man do you think I am? Furthermore, Lord Parkington is the last person whose orders I would ever follow. What a donkey he is."

"But if following his orders were the only way you could stay in my father's good graces, you might—"

"No," he said flatly. He frowned at Emma, wondering what kind of men she'd met in her life before he'd come along. He took her hand. "You have to understand. Soldiers may do things in battle that would be wicked if they were done anywhere else. But we know the difference between our duty to our country, and causing harm to others for private reasons. A good man listens to his conscience, no matter where he is or what he stands to gain. Otherwise, he's not a good man."

Emma looked thoughtful as she absorbed his words. Finally she said, "I wonder if my father—" She cut off the thought.

He waited some more. How could anyone live comfortably, believing that there was no right or wrong, no black and white—only shades of gray? To be sure, the world was a complicated place. In the end, a man's job was to decide where to draw the line that he would not cross.

When she didn't go on, he said, "By all that's holy, I swear that I'd never do wrong just to help me own self." Killian shook his head. "Also, I like Talleyrand, and would never harm the old fellow. "

He watched the doubt clear out of Emma's eyes and the tension drain away. "Oh I'm very glad. I like Monsieur Talleyrand too. Is he in danger? I don't want him to be to be assassinated just because he's a nuisance."

Killian laughed in disbelief. "That's not a reason to assassinate anyone."

"But you know what I mean. I'm sorry that I ever believed you would be capable of such an act. But there are those who will do anything. I can't stand knowing that someone I like is in danger, and their life hangs by a thread."

He sighed. "All our lives are hanging by a thread. There's no telling what fate will bring to us all—you, me, or Talleyrand. Soldiers know this only too well. We are given our time here on earth and we can have no more than that. Life is short and moments of joy are fleeting."

Emma looked down at her hands. "I know. I'm sorry I didn't trust you."

He placed his hand over her folded ones. "I understand. And because time is so short, I want to take one moment of joy with you."

Gently taking one of her hands in his, he lifted it to his lips. He kissed her hand, watching for her response. She turned to him, looking into his eyes, and laid her other hand on his sleeve. Welcoming him. Drawing closer to him. His heart beat faster. They were face to face, closer even the when they had been waltzing. He leaned toward her, delicate as if he were approaching a startled bird, giving her the opportunity to pull away. He held completely still, waiting for her next move.

Drawing in a shaky breath, she lifted her lips to his. For a moment, their breaths mingled. Then he closed the distance, touching his lips to her soft and willing mouth.

He had won. She was his. Desire flooded through him, hot and fierce, and he wrapped his arms around her. She slid her arms around his back, drawing him close. He kissed her again and again, scorched by her sweet flame.

She drew back for breath, and he loosened his embrace, searching her eyes with his. He didn't say anything, not wanting to break the spell.

"I don't want this moment to end," she whispered. "Let's stay here forever."

He tenderly stroked a strand of her dark hair off her face. "There are no guarantees in a soldier's life, but I promise you that I will do all I can to bring about many more moments of joy between us."

"But what if you can't?" Emma's small hands tightened on his jacket.

"Then I will treasure this moment always." She looked up at him, so desirable and so willing to trust in his claim that he was a good man. Her eyes were wide and her lips were slightly parted. Sometimes it was a hard, hard thing to be a good man. With a sigh of regret, Killian stood up and held out his hand to her. "We'd better keep looking."

She looked flustered, but she took his hand and rose from the bench. "Oh, that's right. We must catch that awful Lord Parkington."

They continued silently into the heart of the maze, their hands joined. The turnings became sharper and the path more curving, showing that they were nearing the center.

"Maybe we don't have to find him," Emma said suddenly. "Maybe somebody else can do it. I don't really care what's become of him. Maybe he is just gone."

"No," Killian replied, looking ahead to the opening that signaled the very center of the maze. "A fellow like that is bound to have more tricks up his sleeve. We must keep going until we find—"

The hedges opened onto a small gravel circle marking the center of the maze. A small round folly, composed of a pretty marble dome resting on four Corinthian columns, stood over a marble bench. The breeze had all but died down, and it was completely quiet in the small retreat.

But Killian and Emma weren't alone. Lying stretched out

on the marble bench was Baroness Olga. She was as pale as marble, and she was dead.

Emma looked down at Baroness Olga's still face, pale and cold as the marble bench she rested on. She lay on her back, arms spread wide. Her hair was tumbled about her face, and the turban she'd worn had been unwound and hung like a silken scarf tossed carelessly on the bench.   The giant diamond that had nestled in its folds was gone.

She placed her fingers on Baroness Olga's wrist to determine if there was a pulse, but there was none. "We must tell Lord Castlereagh immediately," she said. She took a deep breath. "I'll stay here and you summon help."

"I don't know my way out of the maze," Killian pointed out. "We can both go."

That sounded shockingly callous. They couldn't just leave her here. "And leave her here all alone? No, no, I'll go."

"Wait—"

Emma was running out of the maze before he could argue any more. It was childish of her, but she didn't want to stay there alone next to a dead woman. And she needed to get away, to think about all that had happened between Killian and herself.

Yes, he was handsome, clever, sensitive, intelligent, and a delight to be with. He set her heart singing whenever he came near. With great passion and sincerity, he had just sworn to her that he was a good man. But he was also a hot-tempered, hot-blooded man, a soldier and a spy. Her heart trusted him implicitly. But her mind urged caution. Life was not so simple as black and white, good and bad. How long did it take to know a man's true character? They had known each other for such a short time.

And there were more immediate questions to consider. Who could have killed Baroness Olga? Lord Parkington had been up in Lord Castlereagh's bedroom, and once he had been discovered, he would have had to run straight for the back gate in order to escape before the footmen caught up to him.

The Prussian could have done it—she hadn't seen him

since the beginning of the ball, and he was ruthless enough to kill. Perhaps there was some reason why the Prussian government wanted the Regent Diamond.

Could Monsieur Talleyrand have killed her? He was there at the ball, and Fiona and Leary were supposed to have told him about the Regent Diamond being here as well. That might have been reason enough. But the thought of the elderly gentleman, with his poor health and his painful limping gait, struggling all the way out to the garden maze made her dismiss that notion. Dorothea of Courtland was young and strong enough—but what reason would she have to hurt Baroness Olga? A rival in love? A desire to obtain the jewel? Some political impulse, perhaps?

She just couldn't think. All she could do was to find her way back to the house and beg for help from Lord Castlereagh. She exited the maze and flew down the gravel pathway, stone spraying out from under her feet. She ran up to the nearest French door, but it was locked and no one heard her knocking. Frantic, she ran to a small side gate and looked around.

"*Was ist los*, Fräulein Forgall?" came the Prussian's familiar voice. "May I be of assistance?"

"Oh, Herr von Hentzow, thank goodness I've found someone," Emma said. "I'm looking for Lord Castlereagh, There's been a terrible—something's happened and I must inform him directly."

"Calm yourself. You are too agitated. Here, come with me," he said. He took her hand and began to lead her across the terrace.

She dug in her heels and tried to pull her hand free. "But I have to tell Lord Castlereagh—"

His grip proved unbreakable. "No, leave that to others. You will come to see what I have to show you."

"Let me go. Baroness Olga—"

"Shh. You must learn to do as I say," he chided her, in the same tone he might use to a disobedient pet. "Come."

He half-dragged her down the stone steps, past the ballroom where sounds of conversation and music could still be heard. He drew her through a wrought iron gate to a small alley, where an old-fashioned carriage stood waiting. One of the two horses turned its head to look at them as they came nearer. The carriage driver, cloaked and hatted, did not turn.

"What are you doing? I am not going anywhere with you," Emma declared loudly, and the carriage lurched, as if someone inside it had moved at the sound of her voice. No one in the house could hear her over the roar of the party. No one lingered in the garden, or stood in the lane, where they might have heard. It was only her, and von Hentzow, and whoever might be in the carriage.

Von Hentzow opened the carriage door. The lantern hanging on the side of the vehicle shed enough light to see inside. It held one occupant—a man, bound and gagged. He lifted his head. She recognized her father.

She drew in a breath to scream, and felt the point of a dagger prick her ribs.

"Now, now," the Prussian said. "No more noise. It is too annoying on the ears."

Heedless of the dagger, Emma threw all her weight against him in a desperate struggle to free herself. She used her elbows, feet, teeth, anything she could think to fight with. "No! Stop. I won't."

She landed a lucky blow on some soft part, and he groaned. "*Verdammt,*" he cursed. Then something hard struck her head. Pain blossomed and she slid into unconsciousness.

15

The wait had been difficult, but after a long, silent vigil beside Baroness Olga's body, Killian heard the sounds of help arriving. Leading the group were Leary and Fiona. They were followed by a number of gardeners and a young footman, who had to be excused shortly after seeing his first corpse. The men gathered around the body and set to work.

"Young 'uns these days," a grizzled old fellow told Killian, shaking his head over the young footman's rush into a nearby hedgerow. "Ain't got no bottom, sir, none at all."

"He'll learn," Killian said. "You don't sound like a Frenchman."

"Naw, sir, I'm from home, came with the Gov'nor on account of the 'orses. He don't trust 'em with nobody but me, y'see, so I'm here with these Frenchies for now."

Killian nodded. He looked the stable hand over. The fellow had bright, sharp eyes and an inquisitive manner. Rather like an old squirrel, he thought. The old man helped to shift the body to a stretcher brought for the purpose, then retreated, wiping his hands.

"What do you think about her?"

The old fellow shook his head and sighed gustily. "Dam' shame, it is, for all the lady's a furriner. But then, furriners get up to plenty of nonsense."

"Foreigner? You mean a French woman?"

"Nah, not French. Not her. She's a furriner from somewhere else, she is."

Killian considered the remains of Baroness Olga. "Why do

you say that?"

The man shrugged. "She just has that look."

That wasn't very helpful. But if this stable hand had noticed that Baroness Olga wasn't French, maybe he had noticed other things. Killian asked, "So, did anything unusual happen tonight? Anything out of the ordinary, anything at all?"

"Naught," the fellow admitted after a long frowning silence. "That is, except the carriage what wasn't supposed to be there."

There was no sense in pressing the old man for quicker answers. He seemed to be the type who was willing to tell his story, as long as he could tell it in his own way. Badgering him would only silence him.

"Tell me about the carriage," Killian encouraged.

"Well, sir, there's a side-alley, you might say, near the stables. For deliveries, tradesmen and such. Proper guests go in that there *porte cochère*, and then the carriages is sent 'round back. So this weren't no proper guest-like. Nor the carriage weren't much to look at. Shabby, I call it."

"So it was a tradesman's carriage?"

"No, lord bless you sir, tradesmen don't come in carriages. They have drays, what can be filled with goods and merchandise, as you might say. But this was a carriage where a dray ought to be, if you take my meaning."

Killian was beginning to have a bad feeling about this story. He clenched his teeth against the desire to make the fellow tell his tale faster. "And then what happened?"

"Well, sir, then one of the guests took a lady up into the carriage."

"A lady? Did you see who the lady was?"

"'Tain't my business to be bandying names, sir." After receiving a coin, which he bit and then tucked away in his pocket, he added, "Can't say I rightly knew her name, but she was a guest, too. Dark-haired, pretty as a picture."

"Anything else you can tell me? Did she seem willing to go with the male guest?"

The fellow scratched his chin. "Come to think of it, she was and she wasn't. At first she was a wildcat, scratching and biting. Then he opened the door and showed her something inside, and in she went quick as you please. Then the carriage left, and that's all there was."

The fellow lifted up the back of the stretcher, and trooped away with the other laborers carrying the body. Fiona Forgall hurried along with them, muttering, "There are some things a woman has to do for another woman."

Leary came up to Killian, wiping his hands. "What did you find out?"

Killian shoved his hands deep into his pockets. "Emma's been kidnapped."

Emma's head was swimming as she blinked open her eyes. Gray stone came into focus—the ceiling seemed to be made of it. She lifted her head, but a sharp stab of pain made her relax back onto the pillow. Pillow? She thought about that for a moment, then opened her eyes again. The ceiling was a gray stone vault. Slewing her eyes side to side, she saw that she was lying on a bed in some kind of stone-block room. She was still wearing the apricot silk dress from the party, with its matching slippers.

Without lifting her head, she tried to see more of the room. A tapestry covered one wall, and a iron-strapped wooden chest sat beneath it. A small window admitted light which fell onto a writing desk. Seated at the desk, his back to her, was the Prussian, von Hentzow.

She must have made some sound, for her turned to her and smiled. "So, you have awakened. Very well. As soon as you have eaten you shall begin your work."

"What work? I will not work for you," she spat, but the effort sent more pain shooting through her head. "I can't think straight. What have you done to me?"

"It is your own fault," the Prussian said. "You must learn not to fight me."

He got up from the desk and came over to her. The bed sank on one side as he sat down next to her. He cupped her face in his hand and gazed with a serious expression into her eyes. "I need you, *mein Schatz*. I am sorry to have hurt you, but it will pass. You will soon become accustomed to your new life. It will not be unpleasant, I promise you."

"I don't want a new life," Emma muttered. She couldn't help the tears that sprang to her eyes. "And what have you done to my father?"

"There, there. All is well." He patted her briefly on the shoulder. "Now if you are finished weeping, look what I have for you." With a triumphant expression, he held up the black leather code-book.

Emma reached for it. "Is that—"

"Yes it is, exactly." The gleam in his eyes was so manic, so wild, that her whole body tensed. He tapped the book. "This is the—what do you call it? Single use code book that the Russian army has developed to send unbreakable messages. It does us little good to intercept the messages, because there is no pattern, no history, no depth to rely upon. Each message is sent using a different combination, so we cannot compare a new message with an earlier one to break the many-layered code. But with this book..."

He caressed the book lovingly.

Emma's head began to clear. "Now that you have the book, why do you need me? Simply apply the appropriate code to the message."

Suddenly frustrated, he slapped the book against his opposite palm. It made a sharp crack. "But I cannot! There are other steps, ones that may not be clear to me, but which you would be able to discover. I have learned from your father of your special talent in that area."

She lifted her head to look at him. "And if I refuse?"

"You will not refuse," he said in a soft, dangerous voice that was more terrifying than any shout. "I hold your family in the palm of my hand. Though you might not accept my proposition for your own sake, surely you do not wish to see your father die. Or your brother, though he is not of much value. And especially not your so-sweet little sister."

She felt sick to her stomach. "Leave them alone."

"Of course, my dear. All you have to do is the work that you do best—decipher coded messages. It should be quite a treat, you know. You will be the first non-Russian to read and understand their private communiqués."

She fell silent. It didn't seem as though she had any choice. Furthermore, she desperately wanted to explore that code book. What a triumph for her, to read and understand the innermost secrets of the Russian army! Not that anyone in the outside world would know. But she would know, and the secret power would be hers to use—not for von Hentzow, but for her own nation. For good and right purposes. But she would have to take it one step at a time. First to get him to trust her. Then to find a way to get out safely with the precious information.

First things first. "Very well. I'll do it."

"I knew you would see reason. Now, let me order you something to eat and when you're done, we shall begin."

Killian's gaze followed Lord Castlereagh as he paced back and forth in his study. The need to burst into action was clawing at his nerves, and the pressure building inside him was nearly unendurable. Emma had been kidnapped, and they were doing nothing. Nothing but standing here fretting and talking about what they couldn't do, instead of actually doing something, anything, to find her.

The other men in the room looked concerned and exhausted. The guests had left the party, except for Killian, Leary, and Monsieur Talleyrand. The latter insisted on staying because of his friendship with Emma, but Killian considered the man had an uncanny ability to nose out a drama or a scandal. The discussion had continued for several hours now, and they seemed no closer to deciding on a course of action.

"And Lord Forgall never returned home either," Castlereagh was saying. "My messenger said that the servants at his house haven't seen him since he left to come here."

"So that makes three men whose whereabouts are unknown," Killian said, speaking slowly and clearly so that Lord Castlereagh would connect the dots that Killian had already traced. "Lord Parkington, Lord Forgall and von Hentzow. And we know that Emma—that is, Miss Forgall, was seen getting into a carriage with a man who was also a guest. It's likely these events are connected in some way."

"That is something of a leap in logic, my friend," said Monsieur Talleyrand, who was sitting upright in a wing chair, his aristocratic face as immobile as a waxwork and his ebony cane propped between his good foot and his club foot.

"But we need to start looking for her now," Killian argued.

"And for Lord Forgall, too. The longer we wait, the worse her danger will become."

"I need you here to investigate this matter of the plot against me," Lord Castlereagh said. "This business of a possible kidnapping might have been designed to distract us from whoever planned the charade that took place in my bedchamber, this attempt to disrupt our diplomatic efforts by causing trouble and terror. We can be certain that plot was directed at me. But we are not yet sure there is truly an occasion to be concerned about Lord Forgall and his daughter."

"Glory be to the merciful will of God, it's sure I am that there's occasion to be concerned!" Killian's self-control was beginning to fray. "Lord Forgall and his daughter have been kidnapped."

Leary stepped forward and clapped a big hand on Killian's shoulder. "Whisht now. We're all here to help you. 'Tis right and natural you're wanting to find your lady love, sure and it is. But where in all Paris are you going to look?"

Killian turned to stare at his friend, suddenly stunned by the realization that he didn't know where to start looking. His heart plummeted into his boots. Even if he began with the assumption that the Prussian had kidnapped Emma, where would he have taken her? Paris was a city with over a half-million citizens, plus several hundred thousand soldiers from a variety of European nations. It would take forever to comb through all the possibilities.

Talleyrand coughed politely. "You are speaking of von Hentzow, *non?* He is a handsome fellow who, I'm told, believes himself to be quite irresistible to the ladies. He is rumored to have many lady friends. But he has a sterling reputation to uphold, and one cannot invite ladies of all stations to one's own home for a, well, a private visit. You understand."

"Where do they go, man?" Killian demanded, flinging himself on his knees in front of the old diplomat. "Where does he take them?"

"To a certain flat in on the Left Bank, in the Faubourg Saint-Germain," Talleyrand said. "I know of it because he hires my cook to prepare meals for him from time to time."

"What is the address?" Killian put on his bicorne hat and strapped his sword belt around his waist.

"I don't know," Talleyrand said simply. "I know the building if I see it, but that is all. I shall have to accompany you, and point it out."

Killian paused. "No, sir, that would be exhausting for you. It would be better if I went alone. Can't you describe it for me? I will take notes."

As Killian looked about for a paper and ink, Leary burst out, "Better if you go alone, is it? Put that thought right out of your head, laddie. You are not going alone because I am going with you."

"*Mon ami,* you cannot go alone," Talleyrand said. "If you are right, you will be walking into grave danger."

16

Emma studied the Russian code book with a growing blend of respect and excitement. Encoding a message took several steps – turning the letters into numbers, then breaking the resulting number sequences into equal chunks so that one couldn't guess a word by the number of symbols it contained, then turning the numbers back into other letters according to the proper page of the code book. Without the book, it would be nearly impossible to crack the code. With it, deciphering a message was a simple mechanical process.

"So," von Hentzow said as he settled into the wing chair that was one of the few pieces of furniture in the room she had already come to regard as her prison. "Have you mastered the Russian system yet? Rather a complex beast, I would imagine. Russian minds tend to think like that."

"I should like to study it further," Emma said, making an effort to be calm. "How long do I have before you sell it back?"

"Sell it back?" He laughed. "How foolish do you think I am? If, for one instant, the Russians knew that I had their precious codebook, my life would not be worth *ein halb-pfennig*. Oh, the Russians would give me any astronomical sum I demanded—but I would have approximately three seconds in which to enjoy it. They would certainly kill me on the spot. And they would find you and kill you too, my dear. So be glad that I would never consider selling it back to them."

"Oh," Emma said feebly. "Then what do you plan to do?"

"Obviously, I shall offer my services—well, your services, although you will forgive me if I don't mention your existence—to my own government. They will pay me well for decoding any secret Russian messages they capture. A splendid solution. Good for me, good for Prussia."

She frowned. "For how long? Just how long do you intend to keep me here?"

He shrugged. "For as long as necessary. The Tsar has designs on land that rightfully belongs to Prussia, and the diplomats here and in Vienna will have to send many messages back and forth as the negotiations continue."

"But that could take months! Years!" Emma's heart beat faster and she couldn't keep herself from glancing at the walls that surrounded her. She felt like they were closing in.

"Oh, it will be no problem, no problem at all. And who knows? If you're a good girl," he leaned forward and played with a lock of her hair, "I might be able to make our relationship very pleasant indeed. You could have fine food, lovely clothes..."

She freed herself and stepped out of his reach. "I'm afraid it's a very big problem. And if you plan to keep me a prisoner, I simply refuse to do what you ask of me."

He lunged at her and grabbed her by the throat. The V of his hand slammed into her windpipe, cutting off her air, and his fingers ground painfully into the tendons of her neck. "Then it will not be nearly so pleasant."

Frozen in terror, she stared into his eyes. They were so wide open she could see the whites all the way around the pale blue irises. His pupils were constricted to pinpoints. His lips were curled into a snarl.

Stars swam around in her vision. She couldn't breathe. "Stop," she croaked.

He let her go. Placing his hands on her shoulders, he set her on her feet. Then he let his hands stroke down her arms. "Now see what you made me do. That is not how I wish for us to proceed. Sit down, my dear."

Still shaking from his sudden attack, she couldn't force her limbs to move. He propelled her to the chair behind the desk and sat her down, as if she were a puppet. Taking a piece of paper out of his jacket pocket, he smoothed it open. "Now look here. I have brought you your first assignment. Decode this message, and we will see where it leads us."

She sat numbly at the desk, still feeling the impression of his fingers around her throat. Her brain felt cloudy and she could barely focus on the paper. To calm herself, she concentrated on breathing in and out.

He leaned over her, waiting for her to get started with the work. When she didn't move, he pushed the code book toward her. Finally, he straightened up. "Very well. I shall leave you to your work. But when I return, I shall expect to see progress, or things will not go well for you."

He walked to the heavy oak door, his back ramrod straight and his fur-trimmed pelisse swinging jauntily over his gold-braided military jacket. She heard the iron key turn in the lock as he left.

The snick of the key in the lock woke her from her stupor. Wild with despair, she ran to the door and pounded on it until her fists ached. Next she twisted the handle and shook it as hard as she could. Losing hope, she slid down to the floor and buried her face in her aching hands.

Gradually, she calmed down. She looked around at her prison. The furniture was old and shabby, but clean and serviceable. There was a bed, the desk and chair, a wing chair and an iron-bound chest. A screen stood behind the door, hiding the necessary offices.

The walls were heavy gray stone, as was the floor, and the entire room was circular. She must be in a tower of some kind. She checked behind the hanging tapestry and felt along the walls for a hidden door. Nothing. The window set was high in the wall, a narrow vertical slit that made her think of the windows through which medieval archers shot at their enemies. There was no way out.

She dragged the chair underneath the window, and stood tiptoe on it to look out. Sure enough, she was in a tower. Beyond was green, open land, with trees and rolling grasslands. They were no longer in Paris.

How would they ever find her?

"Captain Killian, you must calm down," Fiona said to him as the sat inside the jolting carriage. The vehicle, moving at a tremendous pace, went over a bump and the jolt made her teeth snap together. She rubbed her jaw. "Monsieur Talleyrand had no way to know that the Prussian would have taken Emma out of the city. At the very least, that footman does seem to know how to reach the place."

"He'd better know. He charged us a small fortune," Killian growled. He looked into Fiona's sweet, earnest face and regretted his surliness. Though he wanted to howl and break things, she was not to blame, and there was no reason to take his frustration out on her. "I beg your pardon."

Leary leaned down from the driver's box and shouted, "We're almost there. Jean-Luc says that the Prussian is staying at the old chateau about a mile up the road."

"Does he keep servants there?" Killian called back.

A brief pause as Leary consulted with the footman, who was sitting beside him. Though the fellow had indeed charged them a hefty sum to come along and provide directions, he had not led them astray. "No, only an old groundskeeper and his wife. They live in a separate lodge."

"Good." Killian looked at Fiona. "Now, when we get to the castle, you'll stay in the carriage and keep well out of sight. Who knows what sort of devils we're dealing with."

She gave him a level stare.

"You'll stay out of trouble!" he repeated.

"I will do as I see fit, Captain," she said primly.

He rolled his eyes, but gave up the fight.

The carriage stopped in front of a compactly-built medieval castle surrounded by a high wall with rounded turrets at all four corners. A raised portcullis fortified the entrance.

Leary halted the carriage within a stand of trees, ordering the footman to watch over it while they were gone. Fiona got out of the carriage and looked around at the clearing, which was dotted with fallen trees and branches. Some of the branches were big enough to serve as stout cudgels. Killian armed himself with a sword and several daggers. Leary strapped on his own sword and picked up a heavy branch, swinging it back and forth.

When they were ready, Leary turned to Fiona, who was sitting on a fallen log watching them.

"Don't you worry about me," Leary said, kneeling down and taking her hand in his. "'Twill be a game of spillikins. We'll be back with your sister all safe and sound before you know it."

"I know you will," Fiona said gently, gazing up at him with pure love in her eyes. "Be safe. My heart goes with you."

He smiled at her, patted her hand, and joined Killian with a jaunty smile. Leary was the very picture of a man going off to battle, secure in the knowledge that his beloved was waiting for him, safe and demure and definitely not planning to leap into trouble the moment his back was turned.

Killian flashed him a tight smile. Perhaps they should have offered the footman an extra reward for making sure Miss Fiona stayed in the carriage. But it was too late to worry about that now.

He stopped Leary with a palm to his friend's chest. "I'll go first, see who comes out of the woodwork."

Leary nodded. "I'll guard your back."

Killian walked toward the entrance to the keep, feeling a prickle as if he were being watched from the narrow window-slits in the walls. He scanned the battlements, but saw no one between their rectangular teeth. The mid-morning sun shone on the green grass that edged the dirt road. There was no sound except birds and squirrels going about their usual woodland business.

He had just crossed under the portcullis when a voice hailed him. "What sort of a thief and interloper would intrude into a man's castle? Oh, it's you, Irishman."

Standing in the courtyard of the chateau, armed with a pistol, was Lord Parkington. He leveled the weapon at Killian.

Killian sneered at him with more bravado than he felt. "So you're going from mountebank to murderer, is it, Parkington?"

Blast it, he wished he had a pistol of his own, and not just a sword. Not that it would do him any good if he did have a pistol—Parkington would have simply shot him the moment he reached for it. His best choice now was to keep the fellow talking. "Ambitious, aren't you? Your fiery apparition was well done, yet here you are, aspiring to even greater criminality."

Lord Parkington laughed nastily and walked closer to Killian as he spoke. "It was an excellent effect, if I do say so myself. Too bad you ruined it by springing the trap too soon. But I will make sure you don't interfere in my affairs in the future."

"Oh, quite an effect. But why, man? What did you think you'd accomplish by such a trick?" Killian asked. "Did you really think that Lord Castlereagh would believe in your silly smoke and mirrors? He's not so feeble as that."

Lord Parkington scowled. "He's a superstitious fool. It would have worked! You ruined it." The pistol muzzle lifted, steadied.

"Where's Emma?" Killian said quickly.

"What?" The muzzle fell.

"Emma. Miss Forgall. Didn't your esteemed master, von Hentzow, tell you he was bringing her here? I doubt if he can understand how to use the Russian codebook, but he knows she can," he continued conversationally.

"He's not my master!" shouted Lord Parkington. "He's merely a tool I've been using for my own ends. Of course he brought Em—Miss Forgall here. And her father is here as well. She will do as she's told, our little Miss Emma."

Killian's grip on his sword hilt tightened. But Parkington was staying prudently out of reach of his sword, while continuing to aim the pistol directly at Killian's heart. Since Killian didn't dare take his eyes off Parkington's trigger hand, he couldn't see whether Leary was anywhere close by.

"So what do you have planned? A quick demise for von Hentzow, no doubt, but what will be the fate of the others?"

"Oh, I don't think I'll share that with you. Let's just say that plans change," Lord Parkington said. "I think I've discovered what I really want out of life, and it's not political power. Too much work. You won't see me spending my time trying to convince madmen and cowards to do my bidding. Or watching my back every blessed minute of the day in case they turn on me, the wretched traitors. No, I prefer a life of leisure, and now I've the means to do just that."

Still holding the pistol in one hand, he dipped the other hand into his breast pocket and pulled out the Regent Diamond. It flashed in the morning sunlight. He admired it, turning it in his fingers.

"Now this is a treasure just as it is, but I know a jeweler in Amsterdam who will pay a pretty price for it. You might say it's a shame to cut it up, but a group of medium-sized diamonds will bring in more wealth than one large diamond. And the Regent Diamond will have disappeared – no more evidence of a crime."

Killian watched the pistol muzzle droop as Lord Parkington gazed at the stone, raptly contemplating his future riches. If he acted quickly enough, he could probably dart in and disable his pistol-arm before Lord Parkington could aim and fire. Probably.

He took one step, and the pistol muzzle snapped up to his heart.

"You didn't think I was that distracted, did you?" Lord Parkington gloated. "Well, this little chat has been a pleasure but it's time for you to go."

Behind Lord Parkington, Killian saw a flicker of movement. He couldn't take his eyes off the wicked black circle of death that was the muzzle of the pistol, but his peripheral vision noted someone creeping closer to the pistol-wielding Parkington. He had to keep talking.

"Wait," Killian said. "You do know, don't you, that the Regent Diamond is bad luck? All the previous owners have suffered terrible misfortune. Ruined, disgraced, died, beheaded by the guillotine—are you sure you want to risk it?"

Lord Parkington looked at him in disbelief. "Bad luck? What kind of nonsense is tha—"

Before he could finish, a small figure darted forward, a heavy branch held in two dainty hands, and hit Lord Parkington on the back of the head. The pistol discharged into the air and he fell forward with a groan.

Fiona dropped her cudgel and plucked the Regent Diamond out of the fallen man's hand. "That will teach you to take what doesn't belong to you. This must be returned to King Louis."

17

The iron keys rattled in her door.

"I've brought you a visitor," von Hentzow said.

Emma looked up from the codebook. She had been working on deciphering the message he had brought her. There was nothing else to do, no novels to read, no way to take a walk, or do anything else. However, the codebook had proved to be stimulating reading all on its own as she compared the number combinations on each page, making a game out of whether two separate codes would result in different, but still intelligible messages. For instance, what if the cipher on one page would produce the message "Come hither" but using a different page would result in "Stop danger"?

She had considered creating her own coded message pleading for her freedom, but she had not yet figured out how to send the message. Or who to send it to. Perhaps this visitor would help her.

She turned. She gasped.

Standing in the doorway at von Hentzow's side was her father. Like herself, he was wearing the same clothes he had worn to Lord Castlereagh's ball. They were now rumpled and worn. He looked tired. In contrast, the Prussian, now wearing a civilian style frock coat instead of military dress, looked rested and well groomed.

Von Hentzow gave her father a small push into the room, before pocketing the key and kicking the door shut. "You are pleased, are you not? You see, I am very willing to make you comfortable."

Emma stood, frowning at her father. "Are you well, Papa?"

"Perfectly, my daughter." Lord Forgall looked away from her, picking an infinitesimal speck of lint from his coat sleeve.

She drew a deep breath. At least her father's cold, composed attitude had not changed. In a way, it was reassuring. Although she wished she could throw herself into his arms and weep in terror, their captor might see her tears as a sign of weakness. Now she was glad her father had always discouraged displays of affection. "Please sit down, Papa. I am glad to see you."

He chose the wing chair, settling himself carefully in its upholstered depths. He placed his elbows on the chair arms and laced his fingers together over his middle. Von Hentzow took up a position behind the wing chair, like a guard. What was she supposed to say? How could she speak openly with her father when their jailer was watching them every moment, listening to every word? She bit her lip, waiting for her father to speak, to lead the way out of this torturous maze.

"And see," von Hentzow said. "As your father requested, I have also brought some champagne to celebrate. This is a special occasion. A reunion, would you not say?"

Emma exchanged glances with her father. Was it a reunion worth celebrating?

The Prussian set the bottle and a wineglass on the desk, and then pulled two more wineglasses from the pockets of his frock coat. As he did, she saw a sheathed dagger tucked into his waistcoat. This was not so friendly a reunion after all —he was still a jailer, not a friend. But she smiled as he poured champagne in her glass.

Her father nodded at the codebook. "I see you've been keeping yourself busy."

"Yes." *I didn't have any choice,* she wanted to scream. *I've been imprisoned and threatened and forced into this.*

"I assume you know your brother was the one who, ah, pilfered the codebook from certain associates," he said.

She cast a quick glance at the Prussian. He didn't look surprised. Clenching her fists together in her lap, she wondered how many other important bits of information had been withheld from her. But it seemed like she was supposed to play along. She nodded.

"A pity that the Regent Diamond had to be introduced into the equation. If your brother had asked for coins, none of this would have happened. But now it appears that matters have developed in an unexpectedly advantageous way. You are here and the codebook is here. With your able assistance, the Prussians will now be able to keep a closer watch on Tsar Alexander, whose increasingly erratic views have proven quite ... disturbing."

Emma's heart sank. "You mean you have allied yourself with the Prussians? Against England?"

She looked closely at her father for any sign of remorse, of conflict, anything to show that he understood her horror at his betrayal. But he was monstrously calm and relaxed.

"A necessary development at this stage of the game," her father said calmly.

"Necessary?" she spat, jumping to her feet. "Game? Is that what this is, a game to you, nothing more? Betrayal of King and country, everything we've ever held dear? You disgust me."

The Prussian's voice cut like a whip. "Sit down, or I shall tie you down."

She dropped back into her chair, burning them both with her scornful glare. Angrily she picked up her wineglass and took a long gulp.

Her father shook his head. "I thought I taught you better, my dear. Emotion always puts you at a disadvantage. You must remain calm at all costs. It was a good thing I never let Parkington marry you—he is too emotional. I fear his long-term prospects are poor."

"Lord Parkington? I would never have agreed to marry him," Emma said. She frowned at her father. Why on earth was he bringing up Lord Parkington now? What did he have to do with anything?

Her father nodded approvingly. "Trusting him was a miscalculation on my part."

"But I thought Lord Parkington was your right-hand man. He knew everything you did."

"Not quite everything." Lord Forgall's interlaced fingers tightened together, the first sign of agitation that Emma had seen. "He turned out to have an unfortunate tendency toward greed. Greed is a great weakness."

The Prussian leaned one elbow on the back of the wing chair. "What your distinguished father means is that Lord Parkington was responsible for stealing the Regent Diamond in the first place. He was planning to sell it to the highest bidder when that hag, Baroness Olga, got her claws into it at the opera."

Emma frowned. "Lord Parkington stole the Regent Diamond—"

"When he was visiting the Tuileries Palace, yes," the Prussian said. "It was a spur of the moment action, I believe. Then—"

"By coincidence, he was to pass it to the buyer at the opera," Lord Forgall said. "Until your hot-headed friend, Captain Killian, upset everyone's apple cart by starting a sword fight. It fell to the floor."

"Where Baroness Olga picked it up," Emma concluded. "But then at the Castlereagh's ball, Baroness Olga was killed."

Lord Forgall continued, "When it became clear that Lord Parkington had not only stolen the diamond in the first place, but then lost it to Baroness Olga and had to remove her to get the thing back, prudence demanded that my support be withdrawn from him. I should have chosen better for you, Emma. Someone far more clever. Someone like von Hentzow, here."

Emma sat rooted to her seat in horror. Her lips felt numb, unable to form the "no" that was clawing its way up her throat. When did her father become so casual about marrying her off to the man of his choice? When did she cease to be his valued assistant, his best codebreaker, the one person he could trust with the most sensitive secrets of the nation—and become nothing more than his pawn, his easily disposable asset?

The Prussian drank deep from his own wineglass, tilting his head back to get the last drop. He stepped around to the desk to refill his glass.

Lord Forgall stood up and reached for the champagne bottle. "My dear von Hentzow, we should have toasted the occasion. Please, allow me to refill our glasses and we shall drink to your very good health."

"Excellent idea." The Prussian gestured to Emma. "Come here, Emma. I feel I may call you Emma, since your father has done me the honor to consider me as your future husband."

Stiffly she rose and came to stand between the two of them. Her father filled their glasses, and the raised his. "To a brighter future," he said.

"To a very bright future!" the Prussian echoed, laughing. He threw his head back to tilt the champagne down his throat.

With a lightning move, Lord Forgall smashed the bottom of the champagne bottle against the stone wall and thrust the broken end into von Hentzow's neck. Emma screamed and jumped back as champagne and blood and shards of green glass flew everywhere.

The Prussian roared and backhanded Lord Forgall, sending the older man reeling. The broken champagne bottle fell to the floor. Coughing and bleeding, he pulled his dagger from its concealed sheath and staggered after Emma's father. Von Hentzow fell onto Lord Forgall, who struck out desperately against his stronger, younger opponent.

Emma dashed over and picked up the champagne bottle, now little more than a glass bottleneck with sharp edges. She turned to help her father, who was losing the fight. Before she could take more than one step toward the combatants, the Prussian sank his dagger into Lord Forgall's chest.

Lord Forgall looked over von Hentzow's shoulder. His gaze met his daughter's. "Emma," he croaked. "I'm sorry."

He fell backwards, life draining from his face. The Prussian braced one arm against the wall, chest heaving as he drew in deep breaths. Emma raised the broken champagne bottle to bring it down on his back, his neck, wherever she could reach with the weapon. Before she could move, von Hentzow whipped around to face her.

He lifted the blood-stained dagger. "You! You will pay for this."

Emma backed up as the Prussian came for her. His dagger was raised and his face a hideous, contorted mask of rage. She jabbed the broken bottle at him, but it did not stop his charge. She dodged behind the desk, throwing her chair down in his path. He swept it aside. Grasping her by the arm with one hand he raised the dagger he held in the other.

Time slowed down and each moment gained a crystalline nightmarish clarity. Von Hentzow's angry face loomed large. She was trapped. She couldn't get free. The dagger came closer. She couldn't look away. Sounds echoed and rebounded crazily, her shrill cry mixing with a booming crash.

Then Captain Killian's hand stopped the blade's descent, and time snapped back to ordinary speed. He tore von Hentzow off of her and flung him against the wall. Emma stumbled backward, panting and shaking but glad to be free. Captain Killian drew his sword and thrust it at the Prussian.

Von Hentzow was quick enough to roll away from Killian's attack, despite his labored breathing and the gore oozing from the wounds on his neck. He pushed himself to his feet, and drew his own sword.

"You will die, you pig-dog," he growled. He slashed at Killian, who parried his blade and nimbly disengaged. Then there was no sound in the room other than the steely ring of blade on blade and the hiss of an indrawn breath as a sword-point slashed through fabric.

Emma crouched against the stone wall, watching with anxious eyes. Captain Killian was no novice at swordplay; she had seen him fight before. But the Prussian, wounded and bleeding though he was, had the advantage of height and weight over his opponent's slim, wiry form. He, too, was a seasoned warrior, and he hammered at Killian with such ferocity that Emma feared the Captain's blade would break under the assault.

She was no expert judge of swordplay, but she could see that the slighter, smaller man was swifter and more graceful than his bulkier opponent. His energy was boundless, his wrist composed of steel cables, and he was quick as lightning to detect an opening in his opponent's defenses.

A sudden scrape of blades, and the two men were pressed breast to breast, growling, before von Hentzow thrust his opponent away. Killian leaped lightly back, then his sword flashed forward. The Prussian lunged forward savagely, and Emma pressed her hands over her mouth to stifle a cry of warning. But Killian had already parried the attack, fighting with the same wild, gleeful light in his eyes that she had seen back at the fight on the bridge over the Seine.

Killian fought on, never seeming to tire, but with a grim smile on his lips. The Prussian hacked away, driving Killian back toward the open door of the room. Emma followed the quick thrust and parry, by turns elated and despairing. Then it looked like both of them lunged at once.

Seeing an opening, von Hentzow lunged forward. But just as he moved, Killian's blade shot out, sliding along the length of the Prussian's sword and passing on to bury its point deep in his chest. Killian sprang back. Von Hentzow stood stock-still, staring at Killian with a surprised look, before his sword clattered to the floor and he sank down, dead.

Emma stared at the Prussian's fallen body. It felt like a thousand years had passed since he had threatened her life, and now he lay in a heap on the ground. Killian knelt down beside him and felt for a pulse. Shaking his head, he rose and came to her. She could see the sweat on his brow, feel the exhaustion that clung to him.

"It's over," he said. "Are you all right?"

"No," she said, and flung herself into his arms. He held her as she sobbed out her terror and sorrow and pain.

After a while, she dried her eyes. "Thank you."

"I'm sorry I couldn't save your father," he said. "I was too late."

She shook her head. "He did what he could. At the very end, he knew he'd done wrong. He was sorry. He said he was sorry."

Killian embraced her again, comfortingly. "I wish I could take away all the pain. Whatever weighs on your heart weighs on mine, my love."

Startled, she gazed up at him. "Your – love?"

"Yes, I call you my love, because that's what you are to me. I love you," he said. "I love the way your smile makes my heart pound. The way you frown when you puzzle over a coded message, your fierce determination to solve every problem. I love the way you assign a percentage to the probabilities in your life. You're the opposite, you're the other half of me, the missing part of my soul. I never want to lose you, because it would mean losing the most precious thing I know of. When I came through that door, I nearly lost my mind at the thought of never again feeling what I feel when I'm with you. My heart is yours for the taking, Emma, it belongs to you."

She gazed at him with wonder. "For you, I would do anything, dare anything. I want to share your adventures. I would go with you, just to hold the map. I love you with all my heart, Killian, and never wish to be apart from you."

Before they could kiss, Fiona and Leary appeared at the door.

Killian looked at them, looked at Emma, and then back at the couple in the doorway. "If you don't have the sense to leave, at least avert your eyes," he told them.

Then he wrapped his arms around Emma and kissed her, long and hard.

18

"And so, Monsieur Talleyrand, we are bringing it to you, to return to France." Fiona pulled a folded handkerchief out of her pocket. Carefully she opened it to uncover the Regent Diamond. It was the size of a small plum and covered most of her palm. She offered it to Talleyrand.

He stopped her with his palm. "*Ma chérie*, I cannot take this beautiful thing. You must give it to Baron Hüe, here, who is used to smuggling the crown jewels of France."

Baron Hüe looked outraged. "Monsieur!"

Emma, watching the little ceremony from a corner of Monsieur Talleyrand's elegantly appointed salon, already knew the story. When King Louis XVIII had learned that Napoleon had escaped from Elba and his army was rapidly advancing toward Paris, the newly installed King had packed up his court and moved to Ghent for safety. The loyal Baron Hüe had been tasked with getting the Crown Jewels of France, a glittering treasure of loose and mounted gemstones including the Regent Diamond, out of the capital disguised in artillery boxes. As a result of a nerve-wracking series of delays, he almost didn't make it out of Paris with the hidden gems before Napoleon's army arrived.

"Just my little joke, Baron," Talleyrand said. "I know you serve your King faithfully. Please do me the honor of taking custody of the Regent Diamond."

Mollified, the Baron received the gem from Fiona's hands.

"That's that, then," Killian said. "What will be done with the diamond now?"

"I shall take it to the Royal Jewelers," Baron Hüe said. "It will be placed in King Louis' new crown for his coronation. It is quite a relief to have the gem returned, since the jewelers have been asking after it and I had no idea what had become of it."

A lean, almost skeletal man with a dour expression on his lean fox-like face stepped out of the shadows. "I was closing in on the evildoers. I had learned that Lord Parkington had stolen the diamond, and had gone to the opera to sell it—"

"Yes, yes, Fouché, you almost had it." Talleyrand waved his hand, not unkindly.

"But then, all pandemonium broke loose," Killian said. "The diamond was dropped on the floor of the opera box and Baroness Olga picked it up—"

"During the demon dance," Emma added. "Rather *à propos*."

"—During a sword fight," Fiona said with a dimpling smile.

Fouché, the King's secret policeman, gave them a sour look. "You caused great difficulties for us."

"But you have it now, Fouché, and you and Baron Hüe can return it quietly." Talleyrand favored them with a brief smile. "Our difficulties have come to a satisfactory conclusion."

"I will not be satisfied until the gem is placed securely on the King's crown, in time for his coronation," Fouché replied dourly.

Leary frowned thoughtfully. "Are ye quite sure the Regent Diamond belongs on the French King's crown? Seems risky to me."

"Risky? Why?" Fiona asked.

"Because, even though it's big and full of sparkles, it's got quite the history, our Regent Diamond does. It's cursed. I've learned a little something about its history from the Baron."

"I don't believe in curses! It's too pretty to be cursed," Fiona said.

Leary counted on his fingers. "First, they say the poor chap who stole it from the mine was killed by an English sea captain. It passed into the hands of old Thomas Pitt, governor of a British fort in India, had to fight off enemies who wanted to kill him for it. We all know what happened to King Louis XVI, poor fellow lost his head. Next, Napoleon had it. He's finally been shipped off to exile on St. Helena, that barren rock in the South Atlantic. Baroness Olga had it, and she was killed. Finally, Lord Parkington had it and he's being shipped back to England in chains to stand trial. Who's to say what bad luck it will bring the next person?"

Talleyrand smiled. "Bah, superstition. I don't believe in it, my friend. All those people, well, they were to blame for the bad things that befell them. They inspired envy and greed in others, or they were greedy and envious themselves. And so, *voilà*, their comeuppance." He wagged a finger at them. "Always live as the Good Book says, and walk in righteous paths. This I may still say to you, although it has been a long time since I was the Bishop of Autun."

"I didn't know you were a clergyman," Emma said, surprised.

Talleyrand nodded. "For a while. But I felt called to a more secular life, the Pope agreed, and so it arranged itself."

Fouché gave a snort and shook his head.

Talleyrand raised his eyebrows. "Monsieur Fouché , perhaps you and Baron Hüe would wish to carry out your mission."

"Oh, yes, I think so," Baron Hüe said, sounding grateful.

Fouché nodded, and gave a sharp little bow.

The two of them departed, and it seemed to Emma that Talleyrand gave a little sigh of relief.

"How can you work with that man?" she asked.

"Fouché ? He is but a necessary evil, you understand," Talleyrand said. "He does provide some useful services to France, and so he will be endured. And when he no longer is useful, well..." He shrugged.

"What will you do?" Emma asked, a little afraid of the answer.

"Appoint him ambassador to America," Talleyrand replied promptly. "It would serve him right."

Pacing up and down the length of Madame Scatha's elegantly appointed parlor, the Duke of Wellington considered the news that Killian, Emma, Fiona and Leary had brought him. Lord Castlereagh sat quietly, watching and listening.

"Disturbing news," the Duke muttered as he paced. He

stopped short and whipped around to glare at Killian, who seemed to be the only person he felt comfortable talking to. "Who knows about this? About Lord Forgall's death, and so on. The French? What of the Tsar's people?"

Emma spoke up, determined to be an equal contributor. "Monsieur Talleyrand knows some of the story, your Grace. And we entrusted the Regent Diamond to him, because after all, it does belong to the French people."

The Duke nodded curtly and resumed his pacing. "Probably most of them will get word of Parkington's arrest. Nothing to be done about that. Anything else?"

Emma stood up. She held out the black codebook. "There is this."

Wellington approached her, took the book from her hands, and leafed through it. "What is this? Russian, I perceive—a diary of some kind?"

"It is a book for deciphering coded messages." Emma explained how the single-use codes were employed, and how using each code only once made messages unbreakable by anyone without this resource.

Wellington looked closer at the book, eyeing it with greater respect. "How did it fall into your hands, my dear?"

"It actually fell at my feet, your Grace—at the opera. It was supposed to be passed to someone else, but the commotion caused by a, well, by a dispute between Captain Killian and another person, disrupted the secret transfer between the two."

"Who were the two?"

Emma blushed, but she told the story she had prepared. "My brother Ernest, Major Forgall, was acquiring the codebook from Baroness Olga, a known Russian operative."

She wasn't going to say that it had actually been Ernest who had managed to abstract the Russian codebook—probably with the help of some unscrupulous female member of the Russian delegation—and was offering it to Lord Parkington in return for the Regent Diamond. But when Baroness Olga ended up with the diamond and von Hentzau with the codebook, Parkington had gone after Baroness Olga to get the diamond back. Once he'd gotten the diamond back, Parkington had changed his mind and decided to leave the world of diplomacy and intrigue using the proceeds of the diamond's sale to start a new life somewhere else.

"So your brother was instrumental in obtaining this codebook from the Russians? Good man. Where is he?" Wellington asked.

Emma looked away. "He has already left the country, your Grace. But, but I'm sure he will be gratified to know of your approval." Ernest was, after all, her brother. She hoped that he had learned his lesson.

Wellington frowned. "Left the country? Why?"

"He was urgently called away after our father's funeral. He has business in England to attend to," Emma said. It was mostly true, she told herself. "And he has no interest in matters of diplomacy."

Wellington tapped the book in his hand. "So, who else knows we have this?"

Killian stepped up beside Emma. "Very few people, your Grace. Baroness Olga had the book, but she is deceased. So is the Prussian. Major Ernest Forgall is retired, and Lord Parkington is in custody. We believe the fact that it has fallen into our hands is unknown to anyone else."

"What about Talleyrand?"

Killian shook his head. "He only knew of the jewel, and not the code book. And the Russians don't know, either. We will use it cautiously at first, to see if the information we receive is accurate or if they are planning to trick us. But we think its secret is safe."

"Very good. Carry on." Then Wellington, the Iron Duke, handed the code book back to Killian and strode out.

"*Mon Dieu*, what is this?" Madame Scatha said. "He has not said what we are to do, and without Lord Forgall and Lord Parkington, who is there to be in charge?"

Lord Castlereagh spoke up for the first time. "I imagine that will be my duty. I hope you will assist me in steering a course toward peace. It is not our business to collect trophies, but to try to bring the world back to peaceful habits."

"Do you think it will be possible, your lordship?" Emma asked anxiously.

"That will be my earnest endeavor," Lord Castlereagh replied seriously. "It will be no easy task, I fear, to handle Tsar Alexander's demands for the formation of a Holy Alliance."

"What is that, when it's at home?" Leary asked, shaking his head.

"Oh, the Tsar's favorite mystic, Baroness Barbara von Krudener, has proposed that Russia, Prussia and Austria club together to force the so-called divine right of kings on their people," Lord Castlereagh said with a dismissive wave of his hand. "Wellington and I found it hard to keep a straight face when the Tsar explained it to us. It's a piece of sublime mysticism and nonsense. I've told the King not to have anything to do with it."

Emma and Killian exchanged glances. Killian said, "I'm sure we can count on you, my lord."

Finally all of the dignitaries were gone, and Madame Scatha had shooed Fiona and Leary out of the parlor, leaving Killian and Emma alone together.

Killian smiled at her. "Well, it seems that we have managed to get through it all fairly well."

"Fairly well, yes," Emma said. She watched his face. They had made it through the tumultuous events of the last few days, and it seemed that the adventure was over. Everything had been settled, tidy stories had smoothed out the messy truths, and now, what? Were they to go back to the lives they had before? Would she return to laboring over her communiqués, while Killian went on to some other hair-raising adventure?

Killian paused for a moment, then said, "You know, we have some unfinished business to attend to."

"We do?"

"Yes," Killian confirmed with a nod. "I believe I made you a promise once, and I wish to honor that promise."

She smiled, puzzled. "What promise? I don't remember your ever making me a promise."

"I told you that a soldier's life offered no guarantees, and that we never know what will become of us."

Her breath caught in her throat. "I remember now."

"Come here." He stretched his arms wide.

Willingly she walked into his open arms, and he enfolded her in his embrace. She pressed herself against him, laying her cheek against his shoulder. A sense of peace swept through her.

His voice rumbled through her. "And then I promised you that I would do all I could to bring you joy."

With her head pressed against his breast, she nodded. He did bring her joy. She had almost lost her chance to be with him, was almost forced into a prisoner's life. *Sometimes,* she thought, *recognizing a person's good character is not a matter of how long you've known them.*

He tightened his arms around her a little. "Emma, will you marry me?"

She pulled back to look up into his face. "Do you promise to let me share in your adventures? Don't think that I ever want to be left behind to wait and worry."

He expression was comically dismayed. "Sure, and I was hoping to stay home and put my feet up from now on."

"But where is the joy to be had in that?"

He laughed, and drew her back into his arms. "Say yes, and I'll spend the rest of my life showing you."

"Yes," she whispered, and found her joy in the kisses of her wild Irish rogue.

THE END

Author's Note

HER WILD IRISH ROGUE is my retelling of the legend of Cuchulainn and Emer of Irish mythology.   Here is a summary of the story:

Cuchulainn (pronounced "Cook-Hullen") is the mighty warrior hero of the Ulster Cycle, an amazingly good-looking young lad who defeated entire armies with his wild berserker rages. After many youthful adventures, he fell in love with the beautiful daughter of Forgall the Wily, Princess Emer, who possessed the six gifts of womanhood: beauty, voice, sweet speech, needlework, wisdom and chastity. However, she declared she wouldn't have him until he completed a series of heroic tasks.

Hoping to get rid of Cuchulainn, Forgall advised him to make the perilous journey to Scotland, to learn the martial secrets of that famous Scottish warrior woman, Scatha. Cuchulainn and his best friend Laeg the charioteer encountered many dangers and difficulties on the way, the last of which was crossing the magic bridge into her castle. After being defeated by the bridge numerous times, Cuchulainn finally succeeded by taking a mighty "salmon leap" over the bridge and thus won Scatha's respect. Scatha taught him all she knew.

Meanwhile in Ireland, Forgall tried to marry Emer off to another man, but Emer took the other man's face between her hands and declared that her heart was given only to

Cuchulainn. The unsuccessful suitor gave up and left.

After many adventures in Scotland, Cuculainn returned to claim Emer's hand. Her father refused, and Cuchulainn had to fight whole troops of Forgall's soldiers—killing all except Emer's three brothers, whose lives she'd asked Cuchulainn to spare. In the end, Forgall died in an accident caused by his own trickery and the two lovers were united. They loved each other for the rest of their days.

Between Duty and the Devil's Desires

Chapter One Excerpt from:

Between Duty and the Devil's Desires
A Legend To Love

Copyright © 2018 by Louisa Cornell

Chapter One

The gentleman was naked.

Needless to say, Miss Elegy Perkins was shocked... and intrigued... and more than a bit put out with herself. In the three weeks she'd pursued and finally run the elusive Earl of Hadley to ground, she'd gathered every bit of information imaginable about him. The fact he slept in the nude had not been offered, even by the most unsavory of her sources.

"Shall I wake him, miss?" the young maid asked. The sly look she gave Elegy indicated the maid had seen Lord Hadley naked before, and more important, she knew Elegy had not. The gentleman sprawled across the worn counterpane stirred and then subsided back onto his stomach with a grumbled snore. *Thank heaven!* Before the girl reached the side of the ancient four-poster bed, Elegy snapped out of her very-naked-male induced stupor.

"That will not be necessary," she replied in her best governess tone. "Please go below and tell your master his lordship requires a hot bath, breakfast, and a great deal of hot coffee, if he has it, and tea, if he does not." *And a thick blanket to cover the splendor of the earl's beautifully muscled fundament.* Elegy fisted her right hand in her skirts. For goodness's sake, it wasn't as if she'd never seen a naked man. She'd never seen one who wasn't carved of marble, but that was completely beside the point.

"But, his lordship never—"

"His lordship is in my charge now." Elegy removed her gloves and her bonnet and placed them, along with her oversized reticule, onto the battered trunk at the foot of the bed. "Please do as I ask... Daisy, is it?"

The maid gave the slumbering lord one last lingering perusal, and with a pout and an abbreviated curtsy, made to leave the inn's *very best chamber*, as the innkeeper had described it.

"Oh, and, Daisy?"

"Yes, miss?"

"Tell your master he need only send men in his employ with the bath and the food."

The maid shrugged and flounced out the door.

Elegy took in the shabby chamber. Anything to divert her attention from the bed. She'd visited a great many inns on the hunt for Lord Hadley, both in London and along the roads between Norfolk, the farthest north he'd been seen, and Town. With its slightly sloped wooden floors, small fireplace, and ancient furnishings the *very best chamber* at the Spaniard's Inn stood as one of the better places his lordship had chosen to hide.

A prolonged snore, followed by a heavy sigh from the bed, stirred her into action. Elegy marched to the lone window. She bit back a curse as she stumbled over a pair of Hessians beneath the window sill. After a few tries and some unladylike shoving, she managed to open the window enough to let in some air. She picked up the boots, placed them by the chamber door, and then set to work gathering the clothing scattered about the chamber.

"What in the name of Prinny's pizzle do you think you are doing?" erupted from the bed.

Elegy gasped and spun around. Garments slipped from her fingers until only one piece of clothing remained. She clasped it to her chest in the hope of slowing her galloping heart.

"Who the devil are you?" the occupant of the bed rasped. He'd done her the courtesy of drawing a pillow across his lap, but that appeared to be the extent of his gentlemanly behavior. Sitting up on the side of the bed, he was taller than she'd first thought. His frame, long and lean, if a bit thin, rippled with muscles—across his chest, down his arms, and... through his belly and thighs. At least the parts not covered by the pillow. That wasn't what had her rooted to the floor whilst she stared at him like an innocent miss still in the schoolroom.

Hair black and silky as a starless night hung well past his shoulders. With an equally dark beard and mustache and eyes the clear blue of sapphires, even if a bit blurred and bloodshot, Lord Hadley resembled nothing so much as a pirate or, if she were kinder, the subject of a Renaissance painting. Elegy drew herself up and squared her shoulders. She had no time for silly feminine frailty. Especially not where this man was concerned. She had a task to perform.

"I find I hear better when wearing drawers," the gentleman said with a sly grin. He leaned back onto the bed and propped himself on his elbows. "If you're not wearing any perhaps you should borrow mine."

"Borrow... What on earth are you— I most certainly do not wear drawers." What had possibly possessed her to give him that piece of information?

"Ah! Well then feel free to don mine if it will help you to hear and answer my question."

"Don yours? Lord Hadley, I assure you, I have no interest in your drawers or your questions," Elegy declared. Earl or not, the man was the outside of enough.

"Then why are you clutching them to your bosom like a spinster's last prayers?"

She glanced down at the item in her hands. And promptly tossed it towards the bed, where it landed on the threadbare rug at his feet.

The earl chuckled, a resonant rumble of a sound. It

irritated her no end. Arrogant *arse*. She'd be doing Lady Margaret a favor if she left him here to wallow in liquor and other harmful pursuits. Elegy, however, had given her word and struck a bargain that would guarantee her financial future for the rest of her life. He'd not shock or scandalize her out of her purpose no matter how hard he tried.

"I have ordered a bath and some breakfast, my lord," Elegy said as she went to the wardrobe and selected a pair of buckskins, a shirt, a blue and gold brocade waistcoat, and a worn, but still handsome blue wool redingote cut-away. Reasonably clean, they would do. She draped them across an old horsehair chair before the fireplace. "Where might I find a clean neckcloth and perhaps some stockings, my lord? It is chilly out and you'll want to dress warmly for the journey."

"Apparently I need to make use of these drawers as I can't have heard you correctly. Whoever you are." He sat up and bent over to retrieve the drawers from the rug.

Elegy turned her back to him so quickly she nearly fell over. To regain her footing, she strode around the room plucking various pieces of clothing from the furnishings. Somehow, she managed to do so and place them on top of the trunk next to her bonnet and gloves without looking at him. Where were the innkeeper's people with that bath and breakfast? The sudden sensation of heat and the faint scent of an exotic masculine cologne shimmered just behind her.

"There is no need for a journey, you know," he murmured against her ear. "I am more than willing to give you what you want here, love."

Elegy shot her elbow back and connected with the hard flesh of his naked chest.

"*Umpf!* Have a care, woman," he gasped as he stumbled back.

A few sharp raps saved her from having to respond. She marched to the door and opened it wide. "Yes, bring it in," she commanded, taking refuge in efficiency and order, two things which never failed to comfort her. "Set the bath up in front of the hearth and build up the fire, please. And the breakfast on the table away from the window."

She glanced around the room. A mistake, as Lord Hadley stood at the foot of the bed in nothing save his drawers, arms folded across his chest and eyes trained on her in a most discomforting manner. Worse, the young men filling the large copper tub with buckets of steaming water gawked from her to the earl and back, their expressions rife with the worst sort of supposition. God only knew why. Dressed in her warmest, sensible grey wool dress, buttoned to her neck, and wearing her sturdiest half-boots, Elegy hardly appeared the sort of sultry temptress she'd been led to believe his lordship favored.

"Thank you," she snapped and waved a hand towards the door. "That will be all." With some foot dragging and far too many backward glances and smirks, the six young men shuffled out of the room.

"Now, Lord Hadley, I suggest you make use of the bath before it cools." Elegy found the screen in the corner and arranged it around the tub with an eye to keeping the heat from the hearth closed in and her ability to see the earl naked out.

A pair of strong hands spun her around and clamped onto her upper arms. Elegy gasped and tried to wrench free.

"Who. The devil. Are. You?" Lord Hadley demanded.

How dare he!

She planted her hands on his chest and shoved him away. "My name is unimportant. I am here to escort you to Macclesfield." Her flesh burned where he'd grasped her. She maintained her composed, ever-practical demeanor even as both mind and body bombarded her with unwanted sensations.

The aroma of fresh coffee, eggs, bacon, and toasted bread wafted from the rickety table on the other side of the bed. Elegy swept across the scuffed wooden floorboards and poured coffee into a large cup with a small chip in its rim. She paused to calm the tremor in her hands. *Ridiculous.* And completely unwarranted. At thirty-two years of age, she'd long forgotten what it was to tremble.

Lord Hadley behaved exactly as she'd expected. She'd steeled herself on the long journey from Cheshire to deal with a rakish, frivolous, dissipate man. Elegy refused to allow him the upper hand. If she did she'd never take it back. She'd risked her reputation, her good name, and her future on this endeavor. Her entire life had been spent in service, in being treated as either invisible or merely useful. He wasn't the first man to put his hands on her. Let him treat her as he would, so long as he came with her. She schooled her features, turned, and head up, traversed the sagging floor.

"Macclesfield?" The earl shrugged into a banyan and took the cup Elegy offered him. After a few sips and a sigh of satisfaction, he eyed her suspiciously. "What is in Macclesfield and why do I need a nanny to escort me there?"

"Your betrothed is in Macclesfield, my lord. Or rather she awaits you at Braemar Hall near Macclesfield, where you have left her languishing for these sixteen months, as well you know." Elegy found a bath sheet and draped it over the screen. She took the cup the earl had drained of its contents and handed him a bar of soap and a flannel. "I am not a nanny. Though I suspect you are sorely in need of one. My services have been engaged to ensure you arrive at Braemar Hall before the end of this month and that you remain there until you are finally and lawfully wed. What happens after that is not my concern. I suggest you tend to your bath whilst I gather and pack your belongings. We have a long journey ahead of us." She tilted her head and met his belligerent gaze with an insistent gaze of her own.

His brow tightened. His eyes shuttered, evincing neither belligerence nor acceptance. His mouth relaxed into an indolent half-smile. "As much as it is against my nature to ever disappoint a lady, I must respectfully decline your kind offer. The only place I am going is back to bed." He handed her the soap and flannel, allowing his fingers to caress hers as he did. "You are welcome to join me... Miss Whoever You Are." He sauntered to the bed, collapsed across it, and clasped his hands behind his head.

"Not even at gunpoint," Elegy muttered as she dropped the flannel and soap onto a chair and stormed behind the screen before the copper hip bath. She snatched one of the buckets the men had left behind and filled it from the bath.

"Your reputation is already ruined, love," the earl was saying as he reached for a pillow and struggled to shove it under his head. "Might as well—what the hell?"

Elegy stood at the edge of the bed and cocked the bucket back. "You can have your bath in the tub or in the bed, my lord, but have a bath you will."

He sat up. "You wouldn't dare." Lord Hadley narrowed his eyes.

Without hesitation she tossed the water over him and the bed.

He leapt to his feet, spluttering. "Are you mad?" He wiped the water from his face and tried to wring it from his utterly overlong hair.

"No, my lord, I am not mad," Elegy declared and placed the empty bucket on the floor next to his trunk. "I am a person who has signed a contract and who fully intends to honor it. What about you?" She'd just doused an earl in bathwater. In spite of herself, Elegy took a great deal of pride in his shock and surprise. She'd rather surprised herself. And she liked it. Especially if it worked. She folded her arms across her chest and waited.

"I cannot believe I am doing this," he muttered as he stomped behind the screen. His banyan and then his drawers appeared across the top of it. "The water has grown cold."

"It happens when one dawdles like a disagreeable child over a simple bath."

"Shall I come out there and show you exactly how much the child I am?"

Elegy plucked the soap and flannel from the chair and tossed them over the screen. A muffled *thunk* sounded as the soap hit something distinctly *not* water.

"Dammit, woman, are you trying to kill me?"

"Of course not, my lord," she assured him as she moved her reticule, bonnet and gloves from the trunk, opened it, and began to pack the earl's belongings. "If you die before you are wed I do not receive my payment."

"I take it back. You're no nanny. You're a damned mercenary."

"Finish your bath, Lord Hadley. We must be in the coach and on our way before eight o' clock this morning if we are to keep to my schedule." Elegy propped her hands on her hips and gave the room a careful perusal. She spotted a leather satchel on a stool in the far corner.

"Eight o—Dear God, what time is it?"

She consulted the dainty lady's watch pinned to her bodice. "Half seven."

"You *are* trying to kill me."

Elegy snorted and opened the satchel as she picked it up and sat down on the stool. She'd merely meant to check the contents to decide if it should go in the trunk or if it might contain something Lord Hadley could make use of, like a razor and shaving soap.

Letters, bundled and tied with faded blue ribbons, appeared to be written in two hands—one set in a childish hand, the other in a florid, lady-like script. She quickly returned them to the satchel. A lady's silver hand mirror and brush, tarnished but with engraved initials still visible. A child's picture book of animals, worn, with charred spots along the top and front edges. A bundle of velvet fabric was crowded into the bottom of the leather bag. Elegy tugged it free. A child's stuffed toy horse, exquisitely fashioned of rich brown velvet and beautifully crafted stitches in gold thread, had a heavy signet ring tied around its neck by another blue ribbon.

What manner of man had the Marquess of Braemar bought for his daughter? Elegy carried no illusions when it came to Lady Margaret. She'd been the lady's governess for over twelve years. She'd known her longer still. What Lady Margaret wanted, she would have. Her father, a wealthy and powerful marquess, acquired for her by any means necessary whatever her heart desired. Even if those means included offering a governess an inordinate amount of money to drag a reluctant bridegroom to Cheshire, kicking and screaming.

None of it was Elegy's concern. She had plans for the money the marquess had promised her. Plans to break free and finally do something worthy with her life. She bundled everything back into the satchel and placed it on top of the trunk. The room had grown quiet. Too quiet.

"Lord Hadley, I am certain the bath has grown cold enough even for you. Do you—" Her governess instincts on point, she focused her gaze on various spots around the room.

The clothes she'd placed on the chair were gone. The banyan lay in a heap on the floor, but the drawers had disappeared. The screen before the fireplace was askew. The chamber door was firmly shut, and the Hessians still rested beside it. An old oak door on equally old hinges, it would not have opened quietly. An inarticulate shout issued from outside the open window.

Elegy crossed the chamber and pulled the screen aside. The flannel floated atop the water. The soap lay in the floor, the bath sheet half in and half out of the bath. She glanced to the window, open far wider now. The curtains fluttered in the stiff November breeze.

"Really, Lord Hadley?" Elegy tread to the window and peered out in time to spy his lordship sprinting towards the inn's stables in his bare feet. "*Tsk!* Ridiculous man." With a shake of her head, she returned to the foot of the bed and put on her bonnet and gloves.

The chamber door creaked open just enough for a young boy of ten or so years to poke his head into the room. He doffed his cap to reveal a mane of shaggy, wheat-colored hair. "Aw'right, miss?"

"Indeed, Tobias," she replied and retrieved her reticule from the trunk top. "He behaved just as I expected." *Save for the nakedness and the improper advances.*

Tobias strolled to the table, plucked a fat piece of bacon from the plate, and bit it in half. "You called it a'right, miss, that you did," the boy said around his purloined pork. "Want me to take care of the baggage?"

"Yes, please." She spied the satchel she'd been searching through earlier. "I'll see to this. You load the rest into the coach, and I'll fetch the earl."

Tobias laughed and jammed his cap back on his head. "I 'spect you will, miss. Poor sod."

Elegy drew the leather strap of the satchel over her shoulder and slipped out of the chamber. After a quick check up and down the dark corridor, she set off at a hurried but cautious walk to the back staircase. Just as she'd been informed, the stairs led to a door which opened across from the side door to the stables. She crossed the cobblestones on tip-toed feet and cracked the loosely hanging wooden gate she'd paid an extra shilling to have oiled to silence.

Her eyes took a moment to grow accustomed to the dim light, but the warmth produced by the horses' bodies and the abundance of hay was a welcome respite from the icy cold outside. Elegy peered down the long row of stalls. An elderly groom stood at the end of the row, cap in hand. He nodded to his left and placed his forefinger to the side of his nose. She moved slowly to join him. The groom pointed across the way to where her quarry hurriedly saddled his horse.

"Hold still, Hector," Lord Hadley muttered as he tightened the girth around a tall, bay gelding. "My bloody feet are freezing. I'm fortunate I'm not out here naked instead of in my bare feet. Damned wench might have hidden my clothes as well as my boots."

"I've seen you naked, my lord. That is reason enough *not* to hide your clothes." Elegy dropped his satchel at her feet and reached into her reticule. "Your boots are in the coach. I suggest you join them." She pointed the Manton pistol in her hand at him and thumbed back the hammer. "We are late, and I abhor tardiness above all things."

*** End of excerpt of
Between Duty and the Devil's Desires (A Legend To Love series)
by Louisa Cornell. ***

About the Author

Saralee Etter is the author of three traditional Regency romances. Her next book, coming October 2018, will be HER WILD IRISH ROGUE. It is part of the A Legend to Love Regency romance series, with a protagonist based on the legendary Irish hero Cuchulain.

She is still working on A SHORT SHARP SHOCK, the first book in a Victorian-set mystery series featuring sleuth Lucy Turner and her friends, William S. Gilbert and Arthur Sullivan.

You can visit her on the web and sign up for occasional updates at www.saraleeetter.com

Author's Book List

Her Wild Irish Rogue
Lydia's Christmas Charade
Her Very Major Christmas
A Limited Engagement

www.ingramcontent.com/pod-product-compliance
Lightning Source LLC
Chambersburg PA
CBHW032251070726
47590CB00016B/2373